Dr. Conkling—

THEY COME AT NIGHT AND OTHER HORRORS

Evil Awaits You :)

By T.L. Beeding

T.L. Beeding

For Jaina, my little stinker

Table of Contents

THEY COME AT NIGHT — 5 -

IT'S ALWAYS SOMETHING — 14 -

THE DEVIL PREFERS DARJEELING — 19 -

MEASUREMENT OF THE BEYOND — 34 -

GREY GHOST — 39 -

NO TALKING IN THE LIBRARY — 56 -

FERAL — 65 -

THE BOY'S HEAD — 70 -

GREED HATH NO PLACE — 75 -

THE SCREAMING LADY OF PITCH ROAD — 80 -

THIS WAY TO THE GOATMAN — 89 -

FROM THE GROUND UP — 103 -

GOOD TO THE LAST DROP — 112 -

THE WOLFMAN — 120 -

ABOUT THE AUTHOR — 132 -

Copyright © 2023 T.L. Beeding.

All rights reserved. This book or any portion thereof may not be reproduced or used in any manner whatsoever without the express written permission of the publisher except for the use of brief quotations in a book review.

Any references to historical events, real people, or real places are used fictitiously. Names, characters, and places are products of the author's imagination.

First printing, 2023.

Front cover image by BetiBup

www.tlbeeding.com

THEY COME AT NIGHT

Originally published in 'Legends of Night' by Black Ink Fiction (2021)

They always came at night.

Calvin started noticing them shortly after Sienna was born. At sunset every night, an unmarked sedan—polished to an ebony sheen—would slowly pull around the corner of the road and park a few houses down. Its engine would fall silent, headlights extinguishing, but the occupants never got out. They remained inside; always two of them. Hidden in shadow by tinted glass. Unmoving. And by sunrise the next morning, they would be gone. Disappeared back into the ether whence they came.

For a while, Calvin suspected they were watching one of his neighbors. The west side of Elmore was typically quiet, but it housed its fair share of crime. It wouldn't have been the first time something sketchy had drawn the attention of inner-city police, either. But something about it just didn't sit right with him. Every time the sedan appeared, creeping around the corner as twilight fell, Calvin's heart would sink. It felt like watching a predator sneaking up on its unsuspecting prey. Never knowing when or how it was going to pounce.

And it wasn't until that evening, after he'd managed to put a very fussy Sienna to bed for the night, did he realize that the sedan's occupants were watching him.

A pounding knock on the door jerked Calvin up and out of his recliner. He'd just been dozing off, watching the news with his feet kicked up and a cold beer in his hand. Several hard days in a row at work had left him exhausted, as it typically did. He barely had time for himself anymore, not with Sienna needing his constant attention now. Calvin had offered her sitter more money to stay longer tonight so he could catch up on sleep, but the young woman had refused. Sienna had been too fussy that day—too difficult to handle. And feeding her had apparently been a nightmare. It took everything in Calvin to stay awake long enough to feed and get her into bed before dragging himself to the recliner. And now, heart pounding from the sudden shock, sleep all but left him. Calvin sighed angrily, setting the beer down and muting the television. He stood and headed for the front door, turning the bottom lock and pulling it open.

Two men stood on the stoop. Suits of inky black absorbed the porch light, fedoras of the same material and color cast deep shadow across their faces. Calvin frowned, having to tilt his head back to look them both in the eyes—beady, watery eyes, rimmed with red and sunken into sallow, broad faces.

With a start, Calvin realized that they were the men from the suspicious black sedan parked a few houses down.

"Can...I help you?"

"Calvin Epperson?" One of them asked slowly. His voice was raspy and hissing. Almost snake-like.

"Yes...?"

"Mr. Epperson, we need to have a conversation." The second one narrowed his eyes, pressing thin lips together into a bloodless white line. "In regards to the whereabouts of your girlfriend."

"My girlfriend?"

"Rhea."

The name filled Calvin's throat with bile. He swallowed down the anger that boiled up after it. "What about her?"

"We know she left the residence and has not returned for at least several weeks. Do you have any idea where she went?"

Calvin shook his head, shrugging. Brows knitting together in a tight, frustrated frown. "How the hell should I know where that bitch is at?"

"You don't know?" the first man asked, raising a blonde eyebrow.

"No, I don't know." Calvin spread his hands, a sarcastic whistle of breath escaping his lungs. "Your guess is as good as mine, pal. But I'm assuming something happened to her, or else you wouldn't be here." He crossed his arms. "So, what is she? Is she a wanted criminal? An international spy? An illegal alien or something?"

The men's expressions remained stony. "Does she have any friends you know of that she might be staying with? Any places that she likes to spend time at?"

Calvin shook his head. "No. She didn't have any friends, and she always wanted to stay home. I don't think she even has family in the area."

"How did you meet her?"

"We ran into each other on the street—literally. She wasn't paying attention to where she was walking and bumped right into me. She looked lost and confused, so I helped her up and asked her if she was all right. Then she started gesturing at me. I thought she was angry at first, but turns out she was just deaf." A mirthless guffaw escaped his throat. "Or maybe not, considering that the FBI—or whoever the hell you people are—is at my door. It was probably an act to get me to feel sorry for her. To take her in. It worked for an entire year, sadly."

"Were you able to communicate with her well?"

"I guess. I learned sign language so I could talk to her, but sometimes it was jumbled. She said some things that didn't make any sense."

"Such as?"

Calvin shifted his feet. "I'd always ask where she was from, but she'd always just say her name. Maybe she didn't know sign language too well herself—she seemed foreign, at any rate. At the time I didn't pay too close attention to it; she was hot, and I was stupid. It was easy to fall for her tricks."

Calvin bit his lower lip, shaking his head. "Whatever she was involved with, it was clearly more important to her than her boyfriend and newborn baby."

Both sets of beady eyes flashed; their nostrils flared, both men leaning forward ever so slightly.

"Baby?"

Right at that moment, from her room at the end of the hallway, Sienna began to whine. Hungry expressions suddenly rippled across the men's pale faces. Their eyes began to dart, glancing around the interior of the living room. Searching. Sniffing.

"Yeah…Rhea got pregnant almost immediately after we met. She gave birth a month ago, then disappeared."

The closest man took a step forward, trying to enter the house. Startled, Calvin blocked his way by grabbing the door, quickly pulling it toward himself. "What the hell do you think you're doing?"

"Stand aside. We need to see the baby. Right now."

"Like hell you do!" Calvin used all his strength to muscle the man out of the doorframe and back onto the porch. He slammed the door shut, turning the bolt and securing the second lock as well before taking a step back from it. His heart began to pound even harder—as hard as the knock that rattled the door in its frame.

"Mr. Epperson, open this door immediately."

"Get the fuck off my property or I'm calling the cops!"

The pounding stopped. Then a heavy slam shook the entire front of the house, splinters of wood exploding from the nailed hinges of the door. Calvin yelped, leaping backward. The bolt lock held, but just barely – the rounded knob came loose, rattling inside its casing. Another slam bent the lock's thick metal prong, nearly snapping it in half.

Sienna began to scream; fear pulsed through Calvin's legs, driving him down the hall at a sprint. She was red in the face and gasping for breaths in between when he reached her room. Little fists were curled tight above her head, visibly quaking. Wide and fearful eyes were fixed on the open window beside her crib—through which a white face and beady, watery eyes were looking back at her.

"Get the fuck out of here!" Calvin roared, running to the window. He slapped a hand against the pane of glass, locking it and ripping down the blinds to shut out the prying eyes.

"Don't touch the child!" came a stern, muffled demand.

Ignoring it, Calvin whisked Sienna out of her crib, hoisting her onto his shoulder and patting her trembling back. He kicked the door shut, locking it just as the front door exploded off its hinges. Urgent footsteps thundered up the hall, shaking the framed paintings on Sienna's wall. They stopped just outside. The inlaid square paneling snapped with a loud crack, a large, booted foot coming through it—without warning this time.

Sienna screeched hysterically, struggling in his arms. Realizing they were trapped, Calvin stumbled across the room and tore open the slatted closet doors. He slipped into the cramped space, pulling down the extra blankets and baby clothes that were stored on the shelves inside. He bundled them up on the closet floor one-handed, holding Sienna tight with the other. The bedroom door snapped, bottom panel falling out in two splintered halves just as he managed to create a decent pile. Calvin's gut sank through the floor.

"Shh, it's okay...it's going to be okay...." he whispered weakly, kissing Sienna's tear-stained cheek. She had gone silent, but was still trembling. He dropped to a knee by the pile of blankets and clothes, slowly peeling Sienna from his shoulder. "It'll be okay, baby—"

Something sharp stabbed him in the base of the neck – then blinding pain shot down his spine. Fluid began to move through his spinal cord, rushing upward, rendering him abruptly numb from the neck down. A tortured scream erupted from his lungs; Calvin collapsed against the closet wall just as the bedroom door flew open. One of the men in black boiled into the room, raising a gun from the holster on his thigh.

BAM!

Sienna's body caught the bullet, ripping her from Calvin's shoulder. Whatever had jabbed into his neck retracted with a painful sting, leaving him a limp and helpless puddle on the floor. With furious effort, he managed to turn his head.

Bloody pulp and a stain on the wall was all that remained of his baby – but it was no longer Sienna. The mouth gaped open, wider than natural; a long, thin needle-like proboscis protruded from the remains of her throat, from deep within a gut that was full of the clear, viscous fluid she had managed to vacuum out of her father's spinal column. It turned Calvin's stomach so hard that he vomited atop the pile he'd created—the pile he'd intended to place Sienna on so he could protect her from the men in black.

The man across the room holstered his gun, striding to Calvin's side. He knelt, staring at the baby's desecrated body, pulling what looked like a pair of forceps and a sample collection bag out of his overcoat pocket. The second man appeared in the doorframe, watching his compatriot closely.

"Confirmed Rhea young," the man beside Calvin stated matter-of-factly. He plucked the proboscis out of the baby's mouth with the forceps. Something bulbous was attached to the bottom of it, within Sienna's gut—something that still wriggled. The man quickly slipped it into the collection bag, sealing it shut. He held the bag up for the second man, who came forward and took it in both hands. He turned on his heel, leaving the room, speaking softly into a device Calvin couldn't see.

"What...is going on...." Calvin gurgled. His mind was beginning to fog, clouding his thoughts so much that he was having a hard time focusing; remembering what was happening. His entire body was ablaze with pins and needles, lifeless from the loss of spinal fluid.

"I'm sorry, Mr. Epperson," the man said, cleaning his forceps of blood and fluids before returning them to his pocket. Beady, watery eyes took him in stonily. "It's classified information, but I'm sure you can make an educated guess toward what happened. Be thankful the extraterrestrial left you and did nothing else—adult Rheas can drain humans dry within seconds. A painful way to die, I assure you." Something clicked. "The least we can do is make that easier on you."

Calvin became groggily aware that the pistol had reappeared in the man's pale hand. He tried to protest, knowing what was coming next, but was too muddled. Too stunned at the ferocity with which his life was spiraling toward an end. Rising to his full, imposing height, the man in black blocked out the bedroom light.

Much like the shadows of night from which they had come.

IT'S ALWAYS SOMETHING

Originally published in 'Cryptids and Conspiracies' by Crow's Feet Journal (2021)

I didn't think I was that drunk. I'd left the party a little unsteady, sure – may have even crossed the lines in the road a few times – but I couldn't have drank enough to start seeing things.

Whatever it was leapt out from the hedges right as I took the exit into Dover. A dark, sinewy little blot that I barely saw in time. It took both feet slammed on the brakes and a slew of curses to get my car to stop. Smoke boiled up from its protesting tires, giving off the putrid stench of burnt rubber. Meanwhile, the creature – or whatever it was – froze in the middle of the tree-lined road. Not moving a muscle as the car screeched toward it.

"Damn it!"

Everything swayed forward – including the waves in my head – then shifted back. After a moment of reorientation, I craned my neck for a look beyond the hood. Other than the rubber smoke that lingered in wisps, swirling about my headlights, there was nothing. Only the ticking and pinging of my car in idle – and a chittering, squealing sound that clearly wasn't related. I must have hit the creature without realizing it.

I glanced in the rear-view mirror, shifting into park. It was well past midnight, and I was the only person on the road. With any luck, it would remain that way until I could figure out what to do. Unbuckling, I stepped out of the car, leaving the door open.

The chittering got frantic. It was clearly some kind of animal; maybe a possum or a raccoon. It sounded like it was suffering. I grimaced, stepping closer. The only thing I could do in that case was put it out of its misery, but I wanted to see it before I did so. Just one quick peek, to know which direction to turn my tires. With another step, I peered around the front bumper.

Finding glowing white eyes looking right back at me.

"What the—"

Its oblong-shaped head tilted back, a slit opening in the center of its face where the nose should have been. Wiry tongue clicking and chittering between pin-like teeth. A hand came up from beneath the bumper, slapping onto the hood. Spreading sticky tendrils across the paint-chipped red surface. It pulled itself onto spindly legs, one of which was caught beneath the tire.

"Holy shit!" I staggered backward, narrowly avoiding the second sticky appendage that reached for me. The world spun; I lost my balance, tripping over my own feet. Sparks showered across my vision as my head hit the asphalt hard.

I couldn't tell you how long I'd actually laid there. Between inebriation and pain, it felt like years, but could have only been seconds. Perhaps even minutes. All I knew was that it was still dark by the time I came to my senses. And that thing was still pinned beneath my car, eyes glowing like candle flames beneath the bumper. Chittering at me when I finally sat up.

"Ugh…my head." I ran a hand through my hair, feeling for blood. Keeping my eyes on the creature. Its weird, worm-like fingers still extended toward me. I scooted back so it couldn't touch me. "What the hell are you?" I shook my head. "Never mind, don't answer that. I don't want to know."

More chittering. It sounded inquisitive. The fingers wiggled slowly, reaching further.

"Dude, stop! I don't want your slime all over me!"

The hand recoiled. I frowned.

"Can…can you understand me?"

More chittering. The oblong head nodded eagerly. Adrenaline rushed through my chest, pulling me to my knees – to my feet. I must have gotten a concussion from the fall…that had to be it. I shook my head again, patting it. Now feeling for a crack in my skull.

"This is insane. I'm insane." A mirthless laugh bubbled up my throat. "Steve must've put something in my drink to fuck with me…yeah, that's it. Acid or…or something." I gestured to the creature. "How else would I end up running over an alien? Or whatever the hell you are?"

Chitter chitter. The head titled. Candle-flame eyes flickering in a slow blink. After a long moment of staring at one another, the creature wrapped slimy fingers around its trapped leg. Pulling. Trying to free itself. Guilt rippled through my chest.

"Hang on, don't do that." I stepped toward my open door. "If you are real, you'll just hurt yourself more."

The thing paused, staring at me. I left the door open and sank back behind the wheel, shifting the car into reverse. Slowly rolling back. Excited chittering made me hit the brake. I sat up straighter; the creature bounded away, injured leg dangling limply as it pulled itself up by sticky fingers onto the stone wall lining the right side of the road. Then it stopped, turning. Giving me one last, long burning look – perhaps a look of gratitude – before leaping off into the forest beyond. I sat idle in the road for a long moment, processing what just happened. Forcing myself to look at my dashboard. It was 1:30. Adding sleep deprivation to my growing list of proof that I was hallucinating, I slammed my door shut, buckled up, and drove home as fast as I dared.

But the morning was no better – and not for anything to do with my health. I slept well, sobered up, recovered from my fall. I ate a good breakfast and had coffee, too. I didn't even have a hangover. Believe me, I double checked all of these things as I sat there on my couch, stunned to silence.

Watching the local news reporting multiple sightings overnight of a strange little creature with slimy fingers and glowing eyes. A demon, crawling through the forest and crossing roads all around Dover. Chittering like some kind of possum or raccoon.

I swallowed hard past the lump swelling in my throat, staring into the empty blackness swirling in my mug.

"It's gotta be something in the coffee…"

THE DEVIL PREFERS DARJEELING

Originally Published by The Chamber Magazine (2021)

It was difficult to see the house numbers through the thick, swirling fog. The grey, musty effluvium had boiled in off the Thames just as Claire Dennings had encouraged herself to set out before evening began to fall. Though light at first, it quickly became an impediment, reflecting the street lamps' light in massive halos of diffuse, sickly yellow. If it was a warning against her illicit endeavour, Claire tried her best to ignore it. There was nothing that could serve to stop her, now that her heart and mind were finally in full agreement.

Her errand took her in the direction of London's seedy underbelly. Painted ladies of the evening, tucked away in dark alleys and corners more frequently the further on she walked, eyed her suspiciously; even piteously. Hoarse shouts of an undefinable nature became more common, from pubs and inside establishments that had no markings as to the natures of their business -- though Claire could make an educated guess as to what that business was. Though danger seemed to be as thick as the fog itself, Claire kept her head down and walked on with purposeful stride. If she had to place herself in its disreputable clutches for a while whilst seeking the answers she was so desperate for, then so be it.

Eventually, a turn down a dimly-lit avenue brought her in the vicinity of the address she was searching for. Claire slowed her pace, peering up at each ramshackle stoop to check against the number she had written down. Upon the end of the road, when her hope slowly began to deflate, she finally caught a glimpse of the abode she needed: 36 Stepney Way.

Claire checked the curled address written on the sheet of foolscap tightly clutched between her gloved fingers, before glancing back up to the dilapidated stoop. A single street lamp with a weak flame was the only source of light, yet the brass numbers tacked to the face of the facade's chipped wood gleamed brightly. A light source of their own. Claire blinked, squinting further. Everything else about the residence was either crumbling or decayed, but the numbers were freshly polished -- a testament to catching the attention of passersby. It was most certainly the right place. With a heavy sigh, Claire folded the sheet of paper and slipped it into her reticule, then stepped through the rusted iron gate and onto the rickety wooden steps. She knocked three times, swallowing down a sudden sensation of being watched.

After several long moments of uncomfortable silence, shuffling footsteps drew Claire's rapt attention. The door unbolted, slowly creaked open -- revealing a handsome woman of middle age with sharp, grey eyes. She was dressed modestly, in sharp contrast with the housing and area she called home. A closed-mouth smile stretched across her face, wrinkling only at the corners of her eyes.

"You must be Claire Dennings."

Claire's heart dropped into her stomach. "How do you--"

"I know of all who seek my assistance, my dear," the woman crooned softly, stepping back and opening the door wider. It led into a rather pleasant-looking entry hall. "Please, come in."

Claire nervously followed the woman through the house, which was just as deceptive on the inside as the owner herself. While condemned in appearance and locale on the outside, the innards boasted of well-bred aristocracy. The entrance hall led into a sizable parlor, which also happened to be their destination. An overstuffed damask sofa sat in the far corner, beside a shapeley window draped with curtains of black velvet. A circular table sat in the very centre of the room, flanked by two wooden chairs and dressed with sheer fabric that hung nearly to the honeysuckle carpeting. Atop the table, a large, unlit black pillar candle stood beside a black-painted spirit board. Aside from these items of furniture, the room was bare.

Chills immediately overcame Claire, freezing her to the floor. The woman swept to the table's opposite side, seemingly as though she were about to take tea with a guest -- nothing more.

"I...." Claire began, losing her words faster than they had attempted to come.

The woman only smiled wider. "Uncertainty is natural, my dear. The unfortunate thing of today's strict Christian values is that it limits our knowledge of what lies beyond the man-made concept of devotion to one almighty power. The ideology that only one exists is ridiculous." She tilted her head. "Tell me; when your darling Albert passed, was it not the supposition that God intended for his time to be up?"

Claire swallowed, pressing her lips together. Asking how the woman knew of Albert would be moot. "Y-Yes…."

"But you do not believe that to be the case?"

"I...do not know what to believe."

"Albert was murdered, was he not?" The woman's eyes seemed to glisten. "Taken not by an act of God, but by an act of Man?"

Tears stung the backs of Claire's eyes. "Y-Yes."

The woman smiled softly. "Then the Good Lord should not be to whom your prayers are directed."

Claire took the lace handkerchief from inside her reticule, wrangling it. Dabbing at her suddenly tear-blurred eyes. It had been an answer she was terrified to hear, yet desperation gave her no alternative. Albert had been her everything. The rock she had laid her foundation upon, the strength that supported her fragility. Without him, life held no meaning. She had prayed countless nights since the news of his death first reached her; since she had been forced to identify his mutilated body drug up from the banks of the river. Prayed for either an end to her own life, or the return of his in some way.

Claire had passed it off as hysterics until she had heard of the woman in Whitechapel who could purportedly summon the deceased. Could give those who had lost a loved one a brief time to say their goodbyes. It came with a cost -- of what type, the gossip never said -- but she no longer cared. One more night with Albert was worth any price to be named.

The woman gestured to the chair before Claire. "Pray, take a seat, young Claire. I believe I can help you in obtaining what you most desire."

Claire slowly dropped into the chair. She set her reticule in her lap, sniffling as the woman struck a lucifer from a pearl matchbox to the side of the black candle. "What must I do?"

The candle's wick caught, sputtering somewhat before taking on a steady flame. The woman shook out the lucifer, discarding it into a hidden receptacle on her side of the table. "We shall find out soon enough," she replied, taking a seat into her own chair. Her hands, slender and manicured, reached across the table. "Take my hands, love."

Claire laid her trembling hands across the woman's palms. The woman's grip was firm -- almost reassuring. She closed her eyes, tilting her head toward the vaulted ceiling and taking a deep breath. "Close your eyes. Focus deeply on dear Albert. Focus on what it is that you want most out of an encounter with him."

Claire did as instructed, allowing her eyes to fall closed. She drew in a deep, shaky breath, filling her lungs with the stale air of the parlor. She brought to focus Albert's face, youthful and bubbly. The face that had charmed her, even as a young girl. It appeared in the darkness of her mind, smiling brightly -- bristling the thin mustache he had proudly grown before his untimely death. She could almost hear his baritone laughter, at some wiley joke or another he liked to recant with her from his visitations to the gentlemen's club. What she wouldn't give for one more blissful night with him, the chance to speak her goodbyes...and tell him how much she loved him, just one last time.

The woman across from her chuckled. "I see."

Startled out of her reverie, Claire snapped her eyes open. The woman across from her looked forward again, slowly opening her eyes. They sharpened, focusing upon Claire with an almost amused twinkle. She squeezed her hands once.

"You wish for the chance to spend one last night with your dearly departed husband."

Claire licked her lips, nodding. "Yes. Desperately."

The woman smiled again. "It is indeed possible, though it may come at a hefty price."

"What price?"

The chuckle returned; low, knowing. The woman sat back in her seat, releasing Claire's hands and stroking her chin.

"I am unsure; his prices vary, depending on the service requested of him."

A chill fingered Claire's spine, forcing her to sit upright. "Who is 'he'?"

"An old friend." The woman reached once more to her side, coming back up with a piece of paper and an inkwell. She dipped the tip of her pen into the jar, scribbling something across the sheet. When she was finished, the woman slid the paper across the spirit board. Claire took it, turning it rightside-up; on it appeared to be a list of instructions. At the very bottom, the last instruction inscribed, the words 'loose-leaf darjeeling' was underlined twice. She looked back up, trying to swallow down the sinking feeling in her stomach.

"What is all this?"

"Instructions, dear Claire. Instructions on how to summon him." The woman stood, licking the tips of her fingers. "He is able to provide you with what you seek, but just remember the most important instruction of all -- the one which I underlined." Her smile turned crooked, just as she doused the candle flame with her fingertips. It hissed ominously into the silence.

"He prefers darjeeling."

***

The entire return trip back to her modest home, Claire read the sheet of instructions over and over. Mouthing them to herself to commit them to memory. Upon returning home, any second thoughts Claire had quickly vanished as she bolted the front door and made her way to the kitchen. Carefully setting the set of instructions on the breakfast table, she lit three tallow candles in a candelabra and set to work digging through cupboards for the ingredients required. Thankfully, she was a lover of darjeeling tea herself, and had several sachets of loose-leaf to choose from. She found one, pulling it from the shelf. Then she set to work boiling a kettle of water, and setting the breakfast table with a full service tray of milk, sugar, honey, fresh blueberry scones and two cups of the finest china she owned. Once the water was boiled and spilled into the china pot for pouring, she brought it and the candelabra to the table and sat without a word.

Claire glanced the instructions over yet again, careful to read every word. Biting back the uneasiness that clutched her heart. Once the tea was steeped and she had worked up the confidence, she grasped the handle of the teapot and stood. Beginning to pour -- first into the cup set at the empty seat across from hers.

"Lord of the Underworld...I invite thee to tea."

She repeated this phrase thrice, as the china cup filled nearly to the brim. She was sure to leave enough room for milk and sugar -- as the instructions made clear. Then she began to pour herself a cup.

"Ah -- darjeeling. And it has the fragrance of a fine quality, at that."

The deep voice startled Claire into a scream. She nearly dropped the teapot, whirling on her heel; catching herself before the ceremony -- and her fine china -- would be ruined. The empty chair was now occupied by a man, angular face cast in attractive shadow from the flickering candles. Golden hair spilled across his shoulders, matching golden eyes as he looked to Claire with an amused smile.

"Dear lady, whyever are you frightened? Did you not mean to summon me on purpose?"

Claire stared at her visitor, quaking with shock. "I-I...I did mean...."

The man rose to his feet, gently removing the teapot from her iron-like grasp. Once setting it on the table, he touched her elbow. His skin was pleasantly warm. "Please, do sit down. You look upon the verge of fainting. There we are."

Claire allowed him to assist her to her seat, into which she sank heavily. Disbelievingly. She couldn't help but continue to stare in silence as the man reseated himself across from her, pouring milk and honey into the steaming cup before him. A polite smile continued to tug at his lips. Once he had finished, setting his silver spoon to the side of his saucer, he put the cup to his lips. The smile then turned satisfactory.

"Perfectly brewed." He sat back in the chair. "Thank you. Darjeeling has always been a favorite of mine."

Claire cleared her throat, too nervous to move. To speak. So many thoughts rushed through her head all at once that it caused her world to spin. She squeezed her eyes shut before opening them again; the man still sat across from her, watching her with the same amused twinkle that the woman in Whitechapel had.

"Does your mind still denounce my existence?" He chuckled deeply, humorously. He took another slow sip of his tea. "A funny thing, the human brain. A finely-tuned machine capable of quite amazing feats, yet malfunctions often due to strong emotion of any kind. I fear I shall never understand it."

Claire did her best to regain control of her composure. She cleared her throat, straightened her spine. Bit her lower lip to stop it from trembling.

"Who...who are you?" She finally found the courage to ask.

The man set his teacup down upon its saucer, brushing a hand through his glossy hair. "I have gone by many names, some of which are rather unsavoury. Some of which are completely false, fabricated by men who cannot tell the difference between fallen angels and true elements of evil." He flashed her a polite smile. "But you may call me Lucifer."

Claire's heart pounded. "L-Lucifer. The Morning Star. God's favorite son."

Lucifer held up one finger. "Former favorite son -- but yes, I am the very same."

"The...the devil himself."

Her guest frowned, golden eyes glimmering in the candle flame. "That is one of the unsavoury names I mentioned. Also a falsehood. Though I may be devilish at times, I am not, in fact, of that species." After yet another sip of tea, the perturbed expression left his face. "But enough about myself. Let us focus on the present." He inclined his chin toward her. "Pray, what is your name, dear lady?"

"Claire Dennings," she responded softly.

Lucifer nodded once. "Claire. And you have summoned me because you wish for a sizable favor; one only which I can assist with. Yes?"

Claire nodded.

"And what might that favor be?"

"M-My husband…Albert Crestworth Dennings. He was slain a fortnight ago." Tears threatened to well in her eyes once again. "During a dispute that he was not involved in, but merely tried to pacify. Slain in cold blood for being a Good Samaritan." A small whimper escaped her throat; she pressed her fingers to her lips. "Pl-Please, forgive me…."

Lucifer shook his head, voice sympathetic. "You needn't ask for forgiveness for a rational emotion, dear lady. Yet, I find myself asking; since it is apparent that Albert Crestworth Dennings was a soul of purity, whyever seek the services of the Lord of the Underworld?" He shrugged helplessly. "A soul as purebred in nature as that goes directly back to the creator."

Claire frowned. "B-But…the woman in Whitechapel…she told me that only you could offer any sort of hope for me. That only you could give me one more night with Albert, for a price."

A knowing look smoothed Lucifer's expression. "Ah," he said slowly, deliberately. He stuck a finger through the handle of his teacup. "I should have suspected."

"Suspected what?" Claire demanded, voice growing stringent.

Lucifer shook his head. "Lilith. She always does like to play sinister little games with humans."

"What does that mean?"

Lucifer's golden eyes returned to hers, brows folding into a look of genuine guilt. "My sister. It is of her opinion that humans are the dregs of creation -- to which, she does have most of a point. But to this end, she cares not of anything else but to bring mankind harm." Lucifer flipped his wrist. "Humanity is the Lord's most precious possession, for which his loyalest of children were cast to the wayside. It is, I fear, quite a long story." Lucifer sipped his tea once again. "Suffice it to say, Lady Dennings, that you were led into a trap. A lamb to the slaughter, as it were."

Claire's heart clenched so hard with fear that it squeezed a gasp from her lungs. "Wh-What do you mean by that? Speak, demon!"

Lucifer's eyes glowed bright, a frown knitting his brows. "Please, watch your language. I am mostly a well-mannered gentleman, but my fury hath no bounds."

Claire sat back in her chair, appendages abruptly going numb. Her chest and stomach followed suit, effectively drowning her body in pins and needles that kept her bound to her seat by no means of her own. She could only stare helplessly as the glow slowly subsided from Lucifer's eyes, returning once more to a dull, golden sheen only lit by candle light.

"Now. What I mean by my words is that Lilith has so cleverly entangled you into a spider's web, from which there is, unfortunately, no escape." Lucifer drained the remainder of his tea, then began to refill his cup. He stirred in more milk and sugar. "However, I am far more merciful than what is written of me." His expression once again turned guilty. "I am unable to provide what Lilith has promised you, nor am I able to revoke the price you must pay now that I have been summoned." He held up one finger, forestalling the torrent of terrified words that began to tumble from Claire's numbed lips. "Yet, it is within the realm of possibility that noble Albert Crestworth Dennings may be able to visit, provided that you present me with the necessary tools."

The numbness paralyzing Claire began to recede, setting her skin to fiery pins and needles. Once she was able to move once more, she rubbed a hand across her forearm. It stung badly. "I...I'm afraid I don't understand."

"It is quite simple, really. A conjuring spell, as old as time itself, is the answer to your conundrum. The required components are easy enough to obtain, through sheer will and some manipulation. Done through my power, summoning the spirit of Mr Dennings will not be difficult." Lucifer contemplated her over the rim of his teacup. "And to that end, darling Claire, I would like to present a proposition."

Claire sniffed, failing against holding back her tears. "You act as though I have a choice in the matter."

Lucifer granted her an empathetic dip of the head. "Granted. However, that does not mean I cannot try to make the deal on even ground. The price is set -- and it is quite high. A life of servitude to me, in exchange for the chance to live one more night with Mr Dennings." Lucifer took a slow sip.

"But as I said, I am merciful. Seeing as you were duped into this contract, I am willing to grant your wish many-fold. As many nights you require with Mr Dennings, at any time. So long as you continue to serve me, and obtain the ingredients for the spell each and every time."

Tears poured down Claire's cheeks. She had known her venture to be doomed from the start -- either by deception or unwillingness to follow through. She had never imagined herself to be in total agreement with all of its aspects, even after being tricked to accept it. Her willingness to persevere into so wretched a life frightened her. But in the end, she would receive what it is she had sought. Many times over. She could only hope now that Albert, once he returned, would not be disappointed in her.

"I...I accept."

Lucifer pulled a lace handkerchief from his coat pocket, standing and moving to her side. Gently dabbing her tears. He grasped her abandoned teacup with his free hand; steam began to rise from it in curled tendrils once more. He pressed it into her trembling, pale hands.

"Drink, my dear. Darjeeling is your favorite; quite good for your constitution."

***

At first, the conjuring spell was far from simple, as Lucifer had claimed. While most items could be found within the man-made wilderness of London -- herbs, animal blood, tallow candles, and of course loose-leaf darjeeling tea -- the most vital ingredient was the hardest of all to obtain. Claire found it easiest with the weakest of society; drunkards splayed unconscious in alleyways, those just stumbling in a brain fog out of opium dens. Foolish and desperate men, easy to enthrall with feminine charm -- which always ended on the point of a freshly-sharpened knife. It took all the strength Claire could muster to drag the bodies to secluded areas, quick enough to perform the dark sacrament before life took its final bow.

But despite the misgivings and guilt she harbored, each time was more rewarding than the next. Each time she finished her ritual slaughters, scampering home to invite Lucifer for tea, Albert came with him. Filling her with warmth and light, loving her as best he could beyond the veil. And each time tea was over, the hunger to host again grew ever stronger. Visceral. It began to consume her, devour her thoughts. She wanted more. Claire soon began to stalk the fog at night, through the slums that first led her to the life she now lived. The more robust and lively made the conjuring spell work better, kept Albert with her longer. She became so incensed to her nightly vigilance that she unknowingly gained many reputations and many names - just as Lucifer had.

It was no wonder, then, that she had always preferred darjeeling tea.

MEASUREMENT OF THE BEYOND

Clop. Clop. Clop. Clop.

Through the persistent deep, ever-present rumble among the rotting timbers and pocked cinder blocks, Dylan heard it coming. Growing louder. Rattling into his bones. He trembled, pulling the tattered blanket up to his chin. Not because he was cold – the world didn't get cold anymore – but because the sound had woken him up from the first restful sleep he'd had in a while. Pounding into his head. A painful reminder of what day had come.

His birthday.

Dylan had done everything he could to avoid it. He'd tried to hide beneath his cot, tucked inside the crumbling space he called a room, filled with wriggling insects and mold. But the sound got closer, faster. It burst through the door, breaking the jagged piece of plywood off its hinges again. Two stumps of wood approached through the dim – *Clop. Clop. Clop. Clop.* Richard always found him; he should have known better than to hide.

"Happy Birfday, Dillie!" A hand appeared, snatching a fistful of hair. Dragging him out from beneath the drooping mattress. "It's that time again!"

"No, please," Dylan screamed. He tried to reach out, to sweep the wooden pegs at ground-level, but was yanked upward too fast. A clump of hair ripped from his head, fiery pain engulfing his scalp.

"You know da rules." Richard's scummy teeth glistened yellow in the weak light. Behind him stood his filthy army, hunger-stricken faces and wide eyes lining the hall. Frightened. "Everyone's gotta do it on their birfday. Ain't no exceptions!"

Dylan struggled, pulling and gnashing, but emaciation got the better of him. Richard dragged him down the hall, behind the procession of gaunt children. Tapping their sticks, metal pipes, and other makeshift weapons against the walls in time to their leader's steps – *Clop. Clop. Clop. Clop.* A herald of doom.

"Please let me go." His sobs were lost to the deadly tempo, tears splashing into the dirt-smeared cement. He tried to drop his weight, letting his bare feet drag, but Richard cared less. He kept pulling Dylan along like a ragdoll, ignoring his protests. Head held high, like the king he had somehow become. At the end of the hall, the children fanned out, lining the walls of the circular chamber. Rapping their instruments as Richard heaved Dylan toward the mildewed post in the center. A chunk missing from one corner of its halfway point. The flaky, splintered surface brushed against his arm. Dylan screamed.

Clop. Clop. Clop. Clop.

"The time has come!" Richard roared, flinging his arms to the cement heavens. Tapping one peg to the beat. "Another Measurement, to appease the ones in the Beyond!"

"No!" Dylan got to his knees, wringing his hands. "Please don't make me do it, Richard! I'm too young!"

Richard lowered his gaze, a wicked smile tearing open his lips. He gestured broadly to the others. "We're all too young, Dillie. Shoulda known that by now. Those in the Beyond don't give no shits 'bout age. They just want pawns." A claw-nailed finger jabbed toward the post behind him. "And if you's is what they's lookin' for, it keeps da rest of us safe. Everyone's gotta do it, Dillie. Them's the rules. You know dat."

Terror rendered Dylan's body weak. He remained on his knees in supplication, trembling. Praying. Wiry arms eventually looped through his elbows, pulling him to stand. Slamming his back against the post. Richard's minions held him firmly in place, forcing him to look Richard in the eyes. Facing up to his fate.

Richard snapped his fingers, drawing the war beat to a close. Silence rang heavily throughout the chamber, among the drawn faces watching closely with bated breath. From his threadbare pants pocket, Richard produced a pocket knife. Flicking it open, thrusting it up for all to see. After waiting a full minute, allowing uneasiness to fall, he began his approach.

Clop. Clop. Clop. Clop.

Dylan winced at Richard's rancid breath, trying to turn away. Receiving a rough slap in return. Richard gripped his chin tight, pulling him back. Pressing his head against the strut. The dull blade rose, scraping his cheek along the way. His forehead. Running through his hair. When it finally met wood, Richard began sawing.

"Please God...please..."

"God is Dead, Dillie," Richard hissed, making his final cut. The wicked smile widened. "But you remain."

"Wh-What?" Dylan's stomach flipped. Cold relief spread through his chest.

"You remain." Richard took a step back, releasing Dylan's chin. Hands rising once again. "He remains!"

Cheering and banging erupted around the chamber. Dylan shrugged off the two holding him, turning for a look at the post. Seeing the fresh mark cut into its corner – just shy of the mold-blackened gash. His knees turned to jelly, dropping him once again to the floor. Once the celebration had died down and the children went about their daily tasks, Richard approached Dylan alone.

"You won't be so lucky next year, Dillie. You's was barely lucky now. You's is almost a man." A thundering boom resounded from somewhere beyond the ceiling. Richard's gaze turned up. 'The ones from the Beyond always need fresh, young blood. Can't keep playin' their war games without it."

"I don't wanna go up there." Dylan shook his head. "Never. I don't wanna play any war games."

Richard's gaze turned mischievous. "You and me both. Why d'ya think I did what I did?" He tapped one peg against the ground. Clop. Clop. "I couldn't let 'em take me. Not to the Beyond. Not for their war games. Ain't my fight and never will be." He grinned. "Besides...what're they gonna do with a cripple anyhow?"

Dylan found himself staring at the short stumps protruding from below Richard's knees. Forever keeping him a cut below the gash in the pole. The same height as Dylan. He swallowed heavily past the lump suddenly swelling in his throat.

"I don't ever wanna fight their games for them."

The grin grew. "I like you, Dillie. I really do. You might be a pussy, but you got some spirit." He tapped his leg again. "Be a real shame if they took you."

"What do I have to do?" He asked bluntly. Heart racing for the first time with hope.

Richard snickered, bringing the pocket knife up. Admiring the dull blade in what little light there was. Tapping his leg in time to the distant blasts overhead – *Clop. Clop. Clop. Clop.*

"It ain't your fight, Dillie. Besides...what're they gonna do with a cripple anyhow?"

GREY GHOST

Originally published in 'Shadows Beneath the Surface' by Dead Sea Press (2022)

A dense fog settled across the foaming waves, unusual for the English Channel this time of year. It blotted the sea and sky in a bleak grey cloud, forcing the crew of HMS *Integrity* to initiate emergency protocols. Navigation lights were activated and speed reduced; even physical lookouts were posted on both bow and stern to peer through the smothering condensation. Radar had yet to identify any nearby craft. By all accounts, the warship was alone in the fog bank.

And yet the low, mournful horn continued to grow louder and closer.

"How many kilometers to port?" Captain Percival Edwards asked into the silence that filled the bridge.

"Approximately twenty-four kilometers, sir."

He clenched his fists behind his back, turning his gaze to the radar technician. "Do you see anything yet?"

The young man shook his head, eyes wide and uncertain. "No, sir. No other vessels but ours."

Edwards sighed, heart beginning to sink. Since HMS *Integrity* had entered the unseasonal blight on its way in from deployment, the bellows of a cruise liner had begun to follow them across the water. It was distant and hollow at first, bearing no clear point of origin within the swirling clouds. *Integrity* had attempted several times to radio the craft—to warn it of their presence and prevent a collision. But its signature never showed up on radar, and no response ever came.

"Radio in to Port Authority at Portsmouth," Captain Edwards ordered the communications officer. "Alert them of our current bearings and situation. Ask if we may have entered the cruise or shipping lanes by accident."

"Yes, Captain."

As the officer carried out the request, the phantom horn returned with a long, single blast. Looming ever closer, from all sides—from the fog itself. Conversation around the bridge hushed. Confused gazes turned this way and that, scanning the roiling fog beyond the foam-sprayed windscreens.

"Sir," the communications officer said, looking up from his monitor. "Port Authority just confirmed there are no other vessels entering or leaving the Channel at present. We haven't entered a shipping or cruising lane, either." He licked his lips nervously. "I also informed them of the fog, but… they told me I must be insane, sir. They have no reports of fog from any other vessels in proximity of the Channel."

Captain Edwards clenched his teeth. "Then they must be blind." He turned to the first officer, standing silently by his side. "Ask Munson if he sees an end to this blasted fog yet."

The first officer complied, lifting the walkie radio he held to his mouth. "Bridge to Munson. Have you any sight of open water yet?"

"It's beginning to clear somewhat, sir," came the crackling response. "Visibility has extended to at least half a kilometer out."

As he spoke, sunlight began to peek through the misty shroud, soft luminescence burning away its smoky tendrils. A collective sigh of relief swept the bridge. Edwards turned back to the windscreen, inclining his chin. "Increase our speed to ten knots." As an afterthought, he added, "And when we're in the clear, place me in direct contact with an official at Port Authority. I shall be more than happy to give them an accurate weather repo—"

The warm sunlight abruptly dimmed. Vapor boiled back up around the windshields, thickening like clotted cream. It engulfed *Integrity* completely, denser and darker than before. The phantom ship's horn returned—this time directly at their backs. The enraged blast vibrated through *Integrity*'s hull, shaking down the nerves of the entire crew.

"She's right behind us!" came a garbled scream over the walkie.

"Hard to starboard!" Captain Edwards barked at the helmsman.

The helmsman pulled back on the brake lever, swinging the wheel hard right. *Integrity* groaned, rudders shifting violently. Edwards steadied himself as the destroyer swerved out of the collision path, throwing the trembling first officer out of the way and pressing himself flat against the windscreen for a look.

Something massive, cloaked by swirls of murk and sea foam, cut through the water where the battleship had been only moments ago. Waves streaming off its bow sloshed violently against *Integrity*'s decks, shoving her aside like a toy in a child's bath. Shoving her back into the thick of the foggy miasma. The captain squinted, cupping hands to the frigid glass. But all he could see was grey, and the expanding trail the mysterious vessel had left behind.

"Dear god... it's the *Grey Ghost*!"

Edwards peeled himself from the glass, glancing over his shoulder. The radar technician had gone pale, looking sickly in his instrumentation's green glow. His protruding Adam's apple bobbed wildly, eyes rooted to the windscreen. "I-It's the *Grey Ghost*, Captain. I know it is!"

"What the hell are you on about, Hobbs?" Edwards demanded. He grabbed a pair of binoculars from the captain's station, bringing them to his eyes and returning his gaze to the sea. Yet for all adjustments he made to the bifocal lenses, he saw nothing. The pursuing ship had disappeared, seemingly without a trace.

Hobbs swallowed again, eyes nearly bulging from his head. A trembling finger jabbed toward the foaming ocean. "Th-That ship, sir. Th-That... *thing*. It's the *Grey Ghost*." The tremble exhaled into a shaky breath, whistling between gaunt cheeks. "She's hunting us!"

Bewilderment drew a frown across Edwards's brow. He turned to the first officer; the man shook his head, spreading his hands in a confused shrug. Edwards took in the other faces on the bridge, all looking just as perturbed. Growing frustrated, he rounded on the helmsman, who was still correcting the battleship's hard turn. "Does that gibberish mean anything to you, Delmar?"

Delmar chewed his lower lip, focused at task. The vibration from the rudder thrummed through the wheel and into his voice. "It's something of an old legend, sir. Told at the Naval Academy to new recruits. 'The big *Grey Ghost* was mighty and strong, until His Majesty's guns came along. One and two hits to the hull took her down—'"

"Stop!" Hobbs cried, melting into hysterics. His skin turned clammy, beads of sweat popping up on his forehead and neck. A bony hand came up in pleading. "Stop, don't finish it! She'll come back!" A pitiful sob shuddered through rubbery lips. "She'll kill us all!"

"Rubbish." Edwards glared back out the windscreen. "It wasn't a fairytale that tried to ram us!" He gestured angrily at the communications officer. "Hail that damned vessel!"

"B-But what if it's her, Captain?" Hobbs squeaked.

Edwards rounded on him viciously. "I'm not speaking to you, Hobbs!"

Uncomfortable silence rang across the bridge. Hobbs sputtered, but the response died on his lips. Captain Edwards directed his glare at the communications officer. The young man—thankfully made of stronger stuff than Hobbs—swallowed, pursed his lips and turned back to his monitor. He slipped the headset on, frantically tapping in a command on his keyboard. Then he keyed the headset to a clear channel.

"Unidentified vessel," he said, voice quivering. "This is HMS *Integrity*. Please respond. Over."

Hissing static came back across the open channel. The communications officer repeated the request—once, twice. Three times. Growing impatient, Edwards grabbed the headset, ripping it off the officer's head. He held the microphone close to his mouth. "Unidentified vessel, this is Captain Percival J. Edwards of the Royal Navy, commander of HMS *Integrity*. We have reached out to you several times over the past half-hour, alerting you to our presence. If you do not respond, we shall be forced to interpret your actions as an attempted attack, leaving us no choice but to arm ourselves. Do you read me? Over."

Explosive percussion came through the static—mechanical dots and dashes, rapid and in sequence.

"Morse code?" the communications officer frowned.

Keeping the headset close, Edwards listened intently. The string of code cut back to static mid-sentence, hissing loudly into the silence. It had gone too quickly for him to interpret. The heavy effluvium continued to thicken beyond the windscreen, draping sinister grey shadow across the skittish expressions of the bridge crew.

"Have we corrected direction toward the coast yet?" he asked aloud.

Hobbs was indisposed, white as a sheet and still gaping out the windscreen, hyperventilating. Delmar finally managed to even out *Integrity*'s path, but kept silent. No one else spoke up. Eventually, the first officer shifted behind Edwards, leaning toward the navigation console for a closer look. "Yes, sir," he responded, squinting at the display. "We've corrected course toward Portsmouth."

"Unidentified vessel, this is your last warning," Edwards growled threateningly into the headset. "Approach *Integrity* again, and we will blow you out of the water. Over and out."

He thrust the headset back to the communications officer, concern closing a cold fist around his heart. He stared at the choppy sea, setting his jaw. Beyond their vision, cloaked by the nebula of darkness, the phantom horn gave one long, single blast.

***

Despite all instrumentation stating they should have made landfall several hours ago, the destroyer never seemed to move. Every time *Integrity* came close to leaving the treacherous gloom, the phantom ship's horn would return— giving one single, long blast. Soon after, its hulking, shadowy form would come cutting across the water out of nowhere, as though the fog itself were attacking. It would cut the warship off and force them back, keeping them confined in the fogbank. Edwards' repeated threats of retaliatory action went unheeded—and unfulfilled, as the warship had nothing solid to target. It quickly became apparent to Captain Edwards that the other ship was not simply lost in the fog, as they were. Eventually, after so many close encounters and hard turns, *Integrity* began to run dangerously low on fuel. Against his better judgment, Edwards ordered the warship to a full stop as the shroud of night began to fall.

At shift change, while the communications officer tirelessly continued to hail Port Authority for assistance—to no avail—Edwards retired to the galley for something to ease his rattled mind. He sat down with a cup of black coffee and a bowl of potato soup, glumly spooning the creamy broth to his lips. In his twenty-five years of naval service, he had never experienced such a thing. Such a sense of unease and dread. No vessel the size of the one that chased them, phantom or not, could possibly manoeuvre in such a way. Crossing their bow from one direction, then reappearing from the opposite almost immediately, at incredible speeds. And without ever fully coming into view. All the while, the tale of the *Grey Ghost* nipped at the back of his mind. He was not one to believe in the paranormal, but it was quickly becoming the only option he had left. He hated to even consider it.

"What was Hobbs going on about earlier, with this *Grey Ghost* nonsense?" he finally asked the helmsman, Delmar, who had accompanied him to the galley.

Delmar considered his own bowl of soup. "I'm afraid I don't know a lot about it, Captain. But I did some research once we'd been told the story at the academy. Apparently, the *Grey Ghost* was a turn-of-the-century luxury liner." He paused to take a bite. "That's not the vessel's real name, of course. No one was ever able to identify her properly. But from what I could find, she entered a thick fog bank on her way out of the Channel during her maiden voyage around 1916. Royal Navy battleships monitoring the coastline mistook her for a German destroyer. Their commanders attacked without warning." He swallowed, leveling his uneasy gaze with the captain. "She sank in fourteen minutes, with all passengers and crew still on board. They didn't even have time to deploy their lifeboats or send a distress signal."

Edwards stared incredulously. "I've never heard of it. How would such a tragedy go unreported in the newspapers? Especially during wartime?"

"I can imagine the Royal Navy wanted to cover it up, what with having killed innocent civilians and all." Delmar shrugged, pushing chunks of potato about with the back of his spoon. "I wouldn't want that blood on my hands, either. Would you?"

"What about the legend, then?" Edwards gestured at the helmsman with his own spoon. "That rhyme you began earlier. What's all that about?"

Delmar pressed his lips together into a thin, white line. "It goes: 'The big *Grey Ghost* was mighty and strong, until His Majesty's guns came along. One and two hits to the hull took her down... forever hunting the fog for British sailors to drown.'"

Edwards released a shaky exhale, dropping the spoon into his bowl with a ceramic clatter. He put his face in his hands. "Jesus Christ..."

"I don't believe in ghosts, sir, but you can't deny what we've witnessed today." Delmar shook his head helplessly. "We've been trapped in this fog bank for hours, going in circles, when it should have lifted by now. Our communications have been knocked out by it, which fog shouldn't be able to do. We should have been docked and debriefed, warm in our beds on shore. But that damned ship keeps dogging us the closer we get to finding our way out." He took a deep breath. "Even if it's a fairytale and we're all having a bout of cabin fever, I've never felt so uneasy in my entire life."

Edwards considered the helmsman closely, unable to shake off his own sense of mortal dread. The academy rhyme—clearly invented to make new recruits nervous—suddenly sounded sinister when compared with the reality they faced. A ghost ship seeking revenge on the military vessels that were supposed to defend it… it sounded ridiculous. But it was hard to dismiss. Edwards took a slow sip of coffee.

"I can't deny that something is out there… something capable of masking their radar signature. And they're stalking us. For what purpose, I haven't the slightest idea." He shrugged one shoulder. "You think maybe it's the coastal patrol pulling our legs?"

Delmar didn't look convinced. "Forgive me, but that's just not possible, sir. Port Authority saw nothing, our own radar saw nothing. If it were some kind of friendly prank, I'd imagine they would have given it up by now. Port Authority certainly wouldn't appreciate it, either." His expression darkened. "Not to mention that whatever's out there doesn't sound like a Navy vessel." His eyes narrowed. "Whatever's out there has made it abundantly clear that it doesn't take kindly to our presence." He took another spoonful of soup, slowly this time. "That bit about drowning sailors in the fog is a little on the nose, isn't it?"

Edwards shook his head, though his stomach turned. "Ghosts don't exist. And even if the story about the sunken luxury liner happens to be true, a ghost ship holds no power against the might of the Royal Navy. We're on a warship, for Christ's sake."

The phantom ship's horn swelled in the distance. Two long, deep blasts—the old maritime signal to abandon ship. A clear and menacing warning of its own. The corners of Delmar's mouth twitched; fingers clenched around his spoon in white-knuckled fear, eyes darkening further.

"If that really is the *Grey Ghost* out there… being on a warship won't save us, Captain."

Awkward silence filled the galley. Edwards chewed his lower lip, a battle between mind and instinct waring deep in his gut. Regardless of what the truth really was, there was only one thing for certain—the lives of his crew were at stake. With little fuel and an obvious threat lurking somewhere in the fog, it was Edward's sole responsibility to get his men to the safety of shore. Ghost ship or not. He pushed himself to his feet.

"We can't stay out here like sitting ducks."

Delmar looked worried. He, too, had dropped his spoon into his half-eaten soup. "What are you going to do, Captain?"

Captain Edwards downed the entire mug of coffee in one gulp with a grimace. He slammed it back down on the table, then straightened his cap. Gritted his teeth. Prayed.

"We're going to Portsmouth, hell or high water. Tonight."

***

Shortly past midnight, the decks of *Integrity* became a flurry of activity. Crew and officers rushed back and forth, carrying orders from Captain Edwards to ready the ship for its brazen attempt to flee the fog. Their heavy footsteps clanged throughout the warship's steel hull, pounding in time with Edwards' heart.

"All hands are in position, Captain," the first officer stated quietly, failing to keep fear out of his voice.

Edwards nodded, peering into the blackness surrounding the ship. It pressed heavily from all sides: an indefinable maw of danger. Somewhere out there was a beast, lurking in the shadows. Waiting for them to make a false move. Waiting to pounce. Edwards had ordered *Integrity*'s engines to remain off, until the very second his order to sail had been given. If their hidden enemy had eyes on them, he wanted to give as little warning of their escape as possible. He gazed at the quiet members of his crew. All on the bridge watched him with bated breath, all with terrified and taut expressions. He forced his own expression to remain placid, for the sake of morale.

"Ready battle stations," Edwards declared. He clenched his fists at his sides. "On my command, bring *Integrity*'s engines online at full functionality—but keep the navigation lights off. Sail at full speed in the direction of Portsmouth." He swallowed once, setting his jaw. "And may God help us all."

A murmur of acknowledgement went up. Edwards paused; Delmar, once again at the helm, glanced over his shoulder, ashen and uncertain. Edwards acknowledged him with a single nod, then closed his eyes and drew a deep breath. It was now or never.

"Full speed ahead!"

His order was repeated quickly into walkies, tapped into computer consoles and shouted across the ship. *Integrity's* engines roared to life, sending a shudder through the steel-plated deck beneath their feet. Delmar opened the throttle to full, keeping one eye fixed on the fuel gauge. The mighty warship lurched forward, sliding through the smooth, glassy Channel.

For a long while, there was nothing but silence. The warship ploughed blindly through the inky blackness, sprinkles of mist rippling off the windscreen as waves crested high off her bow. Edwards instructed the communications officer to continue hailing Portsmouth. The young man called over and over, begging for help. Not bothering to keep desperation out of his tone.

"Mayday, Mayday, Mayday... HMS *Integrity* to Portsmouth, we are being pursued by an unknown vessel. Intent appears hostile. We cannot obtain a clear targeting position for defense. Please send reinforcements if you receive this message. Repeat: Mayday, Mayday, Mayday..."

Static buzzed steadily from the other end of the channel. Edwards kept his eyes on the radar screen, scouring for signs of the other ship or hopefully even reinforcements from Portsmouth—though deep down, he knew there would never be any.

"Kilometers to land?" he asked into the nervous hush.

"Approximately nine kilometers, sir," the radar technician replied just as quietly—someone other than the hysterical Hobbs.

"Speed?"

"Thirty knots, sir. Full speed."

Pinpricks of starlight began to twinkle through the mist. Dim beacons of hope, slowly winking into sight, piercing through the smothering fog. The veil of darkness thinned, tempting *Integrity*'s sore eyes with the hint of open water. The lights of Portsmouth glistened into view far ahead, bright and comforting on the silhouetted horizon. Edwards clenched his fists tighter, knuckles cracking. Chewing furiously on his lower lip.

"Steady, men… we're almost there…."

Integrity's bow passed beyond the mist, cloudless sky finally coming into view. Someone among the bridge crew muttered a prayer beneath his breath, swiftly making the sign of the cross. Yet Edwards remained tense. Fear began to gain purchase in his heart; he couldn't shake the feeling that something was very wrong. That they were being teased with a false sense of hope. But the warship was very nearly clear of the fog bank. Just a little more, and they would be free of the labyrinth at last.

They were going to make it.

The distant lights of Portsmouth—their guide to freedom—wavered. A dark haze snuffed them out one by one, clouding over with dark spray. The fog swallowed *Integrity* up faster than she could move, entombing them once again. A chill fingered Edwards' spine, cold and clammy. Bringing the hairs on the back of his neck to stand on end.

"No… no, damn it!" he growled, battling the tremor in his voice.

"Captain!" Delmar shrieked.

Movement within the fog drew Edwards' gaze to the gloom. Just as the last of the silvery moonlight was devoured by the returning mist, he finally caught a glimpse of what awaited them in the clutches of the dark.

The narrow bow of an antiquated steam liner sliced between the folds of mist; a ghostly grey behemoth, bearing down on *Integrity* at full speed ahead. Her rotting, rusted yellow funnels vomited black smoke—the source of the fog itself. Two jagged, gaping holes in her hull exposed hollow innards, as though clawed through by a gigantic monster. Coal-powered boilers belched hellish flames up between the tears, heating the iron plates and rivets in her side to a red-hot glow. Her horn blasted again—not escaping steam, but the screams of thousands, murdered in cold blood by the sailors that had sworn to protect them.

Edwards clapped his hands over his ears, gaping up at the horrific beast. Just barely visible across the ship's rust-bitten bow, in fresh white paint, was printed a name that turned his blood to ice.

Integrity.

"Open fire!" he screamed.

The bow turrets of HMS *Integrity* thundered to life. A hail of fiery artillery shells ripped through the fog, muzzle flashes illuminating the behemoth ship—through which the bullets sailed harmlessly away. *Integrity* groaned as the *Grey Ghost* ploughed into her side, electrical sparks and hot shrapnel showering from the hull as the destroyer snapped like a twig. Screams filled the bridge, rising between wailing damage alarms and the *Grey Ghost*'s deathly bellows.

The coppery taste of blood exploded across Edwards' mouth as he hit the steel deck plates face-down. He struggled to push himself to his feet, but the bridge bucked like a wild horse as the *Grey Ghost* came through it. The phantom liner's bow clipped his back, smashing him against the crumbling wall. Tearing flesh open. It carried him out to open water through the shattered hull. He tumbled down the bow, hitting the icy waves and sinking beneath them. Inhaling seawater into broken lungs as he was bashed along the *Grey Ghost*'s keel. With excruciating kicks and strokes of broken arms, Edwards managed to claw his way back to the surface.

Screams and shrieking metal pierced the night, amplified in the supernatural mist. Bony, disembodied hands from within the *Grey Ghost*'s gaping hull clawed at the sailors in the water. Ripping at their faces. Pulling out their eyes. Some were dragged aboard, fed to the hellfire within. Others were held below the surface, desperate splashes the last of their earthly acts. The *Grey Ghost* chugged on full steam ahead, dragging what was left of HMS *Integrity* and its crew through her propellers. They chewed furiously at the sea, spitting out body parts and fragments of metal. A bloody, shredded arm landed in front of Edwards. He splashed it away, screaming. Swimming as far back as he could to avoid the deadly, whirling blades as the liner steamed by. Blood and oil sprayed upward against the hull—a fresh coat of paint that dripped from rusted crevices and between the rents in her side.

Edwards could only watch as the phantom ship's stern passed. He glanced up, to the decayed railing surrounding the ship's deck, shrouded by the smoke from her funnels. Thousands of faces stared back at him from the mist: men, women, children. Officers. All bloated and oozing seawater, eyes glowing the same hellfire from within.

And all at once, they were gone. The *Grey Ghost* disappeared into the fog, giving one long, vengeful blast of her whistle. Stars and moonlight peered through the mist as the phantom liner steamed away, casting a beautiful silver sheen across the rippling waves. The distant lights of Portsmouth came back into full view—too far away for Edwards to survive the swim. They twinkled peacefully, mocking him. Just as the *Grey Ghost* mocked him. And as Edwards slipped beneath the icy waves, too exhausted to keep fighting, the fog bank disappeared completely, taking the *Grey Ghost* with it.

Forever to remain at sea, hunting for sailors to drown.

NO TALKING IN THE LIBRARY

Originally published by The Chamber Magazine (2022)

The ancient wooden sign nailed to the wall behind the librarian's desk always struck Hailey as strange. It looked slapped together in haste, made with with rusted nails sticking out at all angles and rotting wood that stunk of decay. The sign was a permanent fixture in the old building, hung at a time the town of Elmwood had long since forgotten. No one could remember when it was placed there – or why. Yet no one could ever bring themselves to take it down. Even though it was hideous and required constant treatment for mold, it remained proudly displayed.

But the strangest thing about the sign wasn't its vague history or Elmwood's over-protectiveness of it. It was the peeling white paint, scrawled across the splintered surface by an obvious trembling hand.

DO NOT SPEAK ILL OF THE BOOKS. THEY CAN HEAR YOU.

It was clearly a wisecrack made by the establishment's founder. A clever way to remind the patrons of the golden rule: no talking in the library. But it was so odd to be phrased in such a way. Like some type of warning – to keep lips sealed for more than just the sake of others trying to read.

Guess they would figure it out one way or another tonight.

Hailey pressed herself flat to the scratchy carpet between bookshelves, peeling her eyes from the sign as heeled footsteps rapped up the aisle on the left. They echoed around the vaulted ceiling, passing the bookshelf she hid behind on their way to the desk by the front door. The librarian came into view between the heavy oak cases, sniffing heavily and pulling open a drawer. She retrieved an alcohol wipe from within, turning to the sign and standing on tip-toe.

Manicured fingers gently pressed the wipe into the divots and cracks in the planks. It came away black; she instantly dropped it into the trash can beside her desk.

"Disgusting," the librarian mouthed silently, disdain pulling her features taut.

Rubbing the remaining filth from her hands, she plucked the parka from the back of her leather chair and slung it across her bony shoulders. Then she pulled the front doors open, to the wintry blizzard beginning to kick up outside. Without looking back she punched a code into the alarm pad, took a ring of keys from her pocket, then slammed the heavy wooden door closed.

The lock clicked loudly into the silence that followed. After a full minute of waiting, there was movement three aisles over.

"Took her long enough to leave."

Hailey tucked her knees beneath her, shimmying her way to stand sideways between the tightly spaced bookshelves. Several slow shuffle-steps later, she emerged into the darkened library's main aisle. Coming up between the rows, Tina brushed flecks of dust and lint from her jeans.

"This place is disgusting," she grumbled, coming to stand at Hailey's side.

"It's old," Hailey remarked, gazing around. The dim streetlamp outside was the only source of light, and it wasn't much. It cast a pale, sickly glow across the leather-bound tomes that lined sturdy shelves on both floors – and across the creepy old sign, too. Like a ghostly presence, waiting for the girls to make a false move. The hair on her arms prickled. "I don't think we should be doing this…"

Tina's brown eyes narrowed into a frown. "You're going to chicken out now?"

Hailey shrugged. Unable to take her eyes from the sign.

"Well, it's too late, now," Tina snapped, stepping around her. She stomped toward the librarian's desk, tugging on pants too tight for her bulky hips. "Mrs. Lackey set the alarm, so even if we wanted to leave we can't. We'd get caught and have our asses creamed by our parents. You'll just have to wait until morning."

Hailey swallowed, watching Tina pull the office chair from the desk. She thrust it against the wall, steadying its wobbling frame before planting one foot on its cushion. Then she hoisted herself to both feet. Fat hands reached for the decrepit sign, grasping it firmly on both sides.

"Tina, stop," Hailey mumbled weakly.

"No," Tina grunted, tugging on the boards with all her might. They creaked, but didn't budge. "This piece of garbage is coming down tonight."

"We're going to get in trouble…"

"We'll be doing Elmwood a favor, Hailey. This thing stinks – just like all the books in this godforsaken place." She struggled, tugging harder. "Ugh, why won't this thing move!"

A heavy slam from the upper floor thundered around the library. Hailey's heart plummeted to her feet; she clapped a hand to her mouth, peering up through the railing above. Trying desperately to see through the thick, swirling shadows.

"What was that?" she whispered.

Tina didn't answer. Hailey turned to find her frozen to the spot, listening intently with wide eyes. Her fingers slowly slipped from the sign as she lowered herself from the chair, eyes fixed to the upper floor above Hailey's head.

"It sounded like something fell," she replied softly. She brushed mold and splinters from her hands onto her jeans, moving around the desk – heading for the stairs. "C'mon. It was probably just one of these shitty old books."

"Are you crazy?"

Tina ignored her, disappearing up the stairs two at a time. After a long pause Hailey followed, clenching her fists nervously as the darkness thickened. Ahead at the landing, a bright spot of light told her Tina had turned the flashlight on her phone to see. Hailey walked faster as the light disappeared between bookshelves.

"Wait for me!"

The light stopped moving just inside the aisle. Hailey reached it in three strides, turning. Finding Tina standing at the entrance, her phone light focused on a book that had fallen from one of the shelves. Its yellowed pages were open, a fresh cloud of dust pluming between them. An

inked illustration filled one of the pages. Hailey narrowed her eyes; once the dust settled, she was finally able to see what it was.

Hansel and Gretel, pushing the witch into the oven.

"How did it fall?" she asked quietly.

"I don't know." Tina took a step forward. Shining her light closer to the ancient pages.

"It's a big one...someone must have left it on the edge of the shelf or something." Another step closer. "Probably some dumb kid, seeing as it's a fairytale." She shut the book with her tip of her toes, expelling another cloud of dust into the air. "Where does this thing belong?"

Hailey glanced at the shelves to either side. A variety of spines, old and tattered, stared back at her from the shadows.

"I'm not sure…this doesn't look like the children's section at all."

Tina pocketed her phone and leaned forward, picking the book up with both hands. She flipped it back open, yellowed pages falling from her fingertips. Returning to the page they had discovered it on. Her cheeks dimpled as she chewed them. "I've always hated fairytales. Have I told you that?"

"No. Why?"

Tina's rubbery lips pursed. "My mom always read them to me at night when I was a kid, then would rag on me about whatever 'lesson' the story was teaching. Red Riding Hood earned me an hour lecture about how I never listened to her and went my own way, like Red did. Cinderella was that I never worked hard enough." Her lips spread into a scowl, tapping the illustration angrily. "But Hansel and Gretel was the worst. Not only was she always on me about my weight, but she was convinced that my 'bad attitude' was because I was apparently studying witchcraft. She'd always tell me that I'd be burned at the stake one day for it." The fingers curled into a fist. "Guess that's what happens when you have a controlling, religious bitch for a mother."

Hailey frowned. "I…never knew that. I'm sorry."

Tina shook her head, shifting the book in her hands. Testing its weight in her palms.

"Whatever. I'm used to it. I'm just going to hear it again tomorrow. And the next day." Fingers shifted up across the pages, grasping the book on either side of the spine. Her face darkened. "At least she doesn't read me fairytales anymore."

Cracks spider-webbed across the ancient spine, snapping as Tina began to pull it apart.

"Tina, don't!" Hailey shouted, throwing up a hand.

Tina didn't respond, but she appeared to heed Hailey's plight. The book slipped from her

fingers, slamming to the floor in another cloud of dust. It took a moment for Hailey to realize her friend was trembling. Terrified. Staring at the open pages. Confused, she leaned forward for a better look. The inked illustration of Hansel and Gretel on the page was moving. Black lines slithered across the time-worn parchment, like snakes through the grass. Rising across the page to form scratchy words; words similar to the ones scrawled across the old sign downstairs.

WITCHES GET BURNED.

The obese witch being shoved into the flaming oven turned her head back, mouth open in a silent scream – but it wasn't the witch at all. Her face was youthful, with a button nose, chubby cheeks and wide brown eyes.

It was Tina.

"What the—"

The pages of the book burst into angry, sputtering flames. Thick, black smoke curled upward, filling the vaulted ceiling in a dark, brooding cloud of death. Flames licked outward in all directions, scalding Hailey's arms and cheeks. She screamed, throwing herself backward – landing on her backside, just out of danger's reach.

But Tina wasn't so lucky. Charred arms, blackened to the gristle and bone, shot from the depths of the hellfire and grasped Tina's ankle as she turned to flee. The girl fell flat on her face, a blast of air escaping her lungs in a scream. The bony hands began to pull her backward.

"Help me!" she squealed, nails tearing jagged lines into the bristly carpet. A few of them were ripped clean from her fingertips.

Too frightened to move, Hailey could only watch as her friend was slowly devoured by the book. Flames lapped Tina's body, singeing hair and cooking flesh. Her screams became sharp, wailing; and then, all at once, they were gone. She disappeared into the smoke and fire, extinguished along with the flames as the book snapped itself closed. The acrid cloud caught in the triangular eaves above dissolved, leaving nothing behind but silence and a bloody trail of scratches and broken fingernails on the floor.

Hailey's throat went dry, squeezing closed as she stared numbly at the cracked leather cover of the book. It lay still, waiting patiently to be returned to its place. Tears burned themselves from Hailey's eyes, a terrified scream erupting from her lungs.

"What the fuck!"

To either side of the aisle, the ancient bookshelves began to rattle threateningly. She scrabbled to her feet, pounding back down the stairs as fast as her trembling legs would allow. She slammed against the front door, searching for the deadbolt to free herself from the nightmare. To her horror, she discovered the door could only be unlocked one way – from the outside.

Swallowing around the lump in her throat, Hailey pressed her back to the cold metal. Above the librarian's desk, the rotting sign and its peeling paint glowed softly, framed by light from the windows. Hailey sank to the floor, clammy hands clamped across her mouth. Staring at the sign and its one golden rule.

Do not speak ill of the books.

FERAL

*Originally published by Tales to Terrify, Episode *578 (2023)*

One of the calves was missing from the herd.

I assumed she'd just strayed too far from the others, lost out there in the pasture by her lonesome. The herd had grazed pretty far from the barn that day, gathering by the perimeter fence separating the field from the woods beyond. But the mother wasn't acting right. She brayed and gnashed, kept turning back to the field. Eyes darting in panic. I searched as far as I could see, along the crest of the hill. Swallowing down dread. It wouldn't have been the first time one of the girls had been jumped by something out there. A coyote lurked in those woods, one that liked to pick at my cattle when opportunity struck. I'd caught it a few times, slinking between the trees with a strip of bloody hide in its jowls. But it had never been successful in its hunting – and I hoped it wasn't now.

By the time I got the rest of the cattle penned, night was beginning to fall. Arming myself with a flashlight and a rifle, I struck out across the field and scanned for any signs of where the calf might have gone. Searching for tracks, manure...anything. I called out for her, sweeping my light across the grass. But there was nothing. Only a gentle breeze that shivered through the corn stalks. Rustling trees in the woods across the way. I shined my light that direction the closer I got, but it never seemed to penetrate the shadow. It was dark and thick, an inky blot against the rapidly dimming horizon.

At the perimeter fence my flashlight revealed a hole in the chain links, pulled apart and chewed off in jagged points. Stained crimson with blood. It was too big a hole to be the wily coyote; it had to have been something larger. A bear, maybe. I aimed my beam of light into the trees across the road, finding a slick, red stain smearing the asphalt leading into the woods. A gruesome path, inviting me to follow. My gut churned. Now that the bear – or whatever it was – had a taste of cattle, it would surely be back for more. I could have left it alone, reported it to the sheriff...but the tracks looked fresh. The creature couldn't be too far ahead.

The trail wound between ancient gnarled trunks, growing clotted the further in it led rather than fading away in the dirt. It streaked the deep drag lines gouged into the earth, unfettered stench attracting biting insects that hoped for more. Along the way, there began to be more than just blood. Tufts of black and white fur speckled thorny twigs jutting from the brush. Bile rose in my throat as I followed the tracks to the edge of a clearing, where I found the underbrush torn from the ground in the narrow space between two trees. Bloody chunks of flesh stuck to the jagged roots and bark on either side, still warm. Still dripping.

A rustle beyond the brush stopped my heart. I dropped the flashlight, hoisting the rifle in trembling hands toward the clearing. Jaundiced light shown in patchwork spots, illuminating the face of a crumbling, rusted facade I barely recognized as a building. Something sprawled across the path before a sagging door frame in a pool of blood, surrounded by bits of jagged metal and rocks. It squirmed and moaned, legs beating the dirt in spasms. Bleating quietly, helplessly.

"Shit."

I stomped through the brush, keeping my rifle close. I could already tell she was beyond salvation, but I wanted a closer look regardless. To see what kind of animal could have done so much damage. I slowed, stomach churning. Finding her belly ripped open, organs stretched the length of the clearing. I found another set of tracks leading into the dilapidated building, stained with her coagulated blood and tissue. By the looks of them, the predator was massive; the imprints were heavy, dug deep into the soil. But they were in pairs of two, not pairs of four. I knelt beside the calf, squinting.

The other prints were human.

Something squelched inside the building. I jerked my head up, staring into the darkness. Heart pounding into my throat. My eyes finally adjusted to find a shadow lurking in the doorway, hunched over the trail of decimated organs. It slurped and grunted, only stopping when it finally seemed to notice I was there. A sickening gurgle emanated from the shadow; a slow, wet suction of breath, rattling deep from the chest. A chuckle. I shot to my feet, shakily raising the rifle toward the dark.

"Show yourself! *Now!*"

The chuckling continued. The shadow rose, filling the entirety of the doorframe. With a vicious pull, the calf's entrails were ripped free, slithering away into the darkness toward the hulking shape. Hot blood splattered my coveralls. The calf gave a raspy scream, flailing one last time before falling still. Then more slurping took up from the building.

Fear iced my blood, driving me back through the brush toward the trail. The flashlight crunched beneath my boot, casting me in complete darkness with whatever - whoever - mutilated my calf. Somehow I lost my rifle along the way, striking every tree and getting stung by every insect in my blind flight out of the woods. The soothing lights of my farmhouse appeared between the trunks, and I barreled for it as fast as I could. I leapt over the perimeter fence and in through the back door before the adrenaline wore off and collapsed me onto the kitchen counter.

I don't know how long I spent catching my breath before I called the sheriff, but it seemed like hours. When they finally arrived they scoured the woods with bloodhounds and flashlights. I directed them to the drag marks and bloodstains, but refused to follow. I didn't want to relive terror like that so soon after. Eventually the police returned, somehow empty-handed. Only finding evidence of the blood and tissue.

"You sure of what you saw?"

"Damn sure." I bit my thumbnail. "It was a man, I'm tellin' you."

"We didn't find nothin' but blood and footprints." The sheriff hooked his thumbs in his belt. "If you say it was a man, then that man's gotta be stronger than an ox. Strong enough to drag a calf through the woods, and away again after you startled him. Did you get a good look at him?"

"No. He never came out of that building. But he chuckled at me. Slurped my cow's guts at me." I shook my head. "Who the hell does those kinds of things?"

The sheriff's face went sour. "If he's feral...God only knows." After a long moment, he clicked his tongue and nodded. "Well, I suggest you repair that fence and maybe get a guard dog. We've had some other reports of animals gone missing lately 'round these parts. We'll keep an eye out a little longer. But keep yourself safe, you hear?"

I sat up the rest of the night in my kitchen with every light on, facing the window that led toward the woods. Scanning each shadow, scrutinizing every sound. Praying for anything to remove that awful sound from my head. The slurping and the chuckling, and bloody soil squelching between bare toes. Praying that I would never witness something so heinous again.

But if that man was feral...God only knows.

THE BOY'S HEAD

Originally published by Tales from the Moonlit Path, Summer Issue (2021)

It was common knowledge that Lord Terrence Hastings had a habit of collecting masks of the strange and whimsical – even the macabre. Most visitors to Whitely Hall (of which there were few) recanted their discomfort at the menagerie; the walls seemed to 'gain life' at night, lit only with eerie incandescence from a single gas lamp in the hall where the lord kept his prized possessions. A haunted house, most called it. If not haunted by true spectres, then by the curious fellow that proudly called such a grisly abode his home.

And as Stuart Langsdale stared up at the pale, gaping face without eyes affixed to the wall, he couldn't stop those ridiculous notions from creeping to the forefront of his mind.

"This is a recent acquisition, you said?"

"Indeed," Lord Hastings replied proudly. The strike and hiss of a lucifer filled the room, soon accompanied by the ashy smell of a lit cigar. "A rarity that I had been pursuing with utmost effort. I call it 'The Boy's Head'."

Langsdale grimaced at the gruesome moniker, forcing himself to turn. "Where did you acquire it?"

Hastings puffed on the cigar, a blue ring of acrid smoke haloing his head. He reached into the pocket of his dressing gown, retrieving a silver cigar case. He offered it to Langsdale, who declined with a shake of his head. "I have a keen eye for such things, Inspector Langsdale," the stout man stated happily, slipping the cigar case back into his pocket. "I acquire my trinkets from all across the globe, as you can see. Some I even create myself."

A broad gesture encompassed the expanse of the wide, dimly lit room. Langsdale cast his gaze about the ghastly menagerie of faces – 'trinkets' that consisted of Plaster of Paris, feathered and beaded faces, painted ones, porcelain ones, and others that seemed to have no explanation. Some smiled, some laughed with open mouths. Most simply stared. But, whilst all were disturbing, there was none more so than the face of the young man.

Langsdale returned his attention to his quarry. "That does not answer my question, Lord Hastings. This 'Boy's Head', as you call it, is why I am here. A rather frantic fellow came to Scotland Yard this morning; we were barely able to get the story from him, through tremors and faintness." He eyed the burly man over his shoulder. "According to him, he was an overnight guest at your residence last evening. He was awoken by a terrible scream in the night."

"Could have been a fox."

"He heard it from within." Langsdale narrowed his eyes. "And when he asked the butler for an explanation, he was told it was of no concern and to return to his room until morning. At which time he presently fled."

Lord Hastings paused to take a long, thoughtful drag on his cigar.

"Are you a married man, Inspector Langsdale?"

Langsdale's frown increased. "Yes, sir. What of it?"

"Do you love your wife?"

"What has that to do with this discussion?"

"I confess that I have never loved anyone stronger than my own darling Charlotte," Lord Hastings continued on, as though he hadn't heard Langsdale's reply. "She was the apple of my eye, classically beautiful and perfectly modest." Puffs of smoke escaped his lips like a chugging steam engine. "Or so I had believed."

Langsdale's ears perked. "Sir?"

The look upon Hasting's face had rapidly changed, within the blink of an eye. Where he had once been full of hot air and rather convivial, his jowls now drooped lopsidedly with gritted anger. Eyes, dark as coal, shimmered in the scant light provided by the room's singular gas lamp.

"Love is fickle, Inspector Langsdale. You would be wise to remember that. Though I suppose the blame is partially mine. I made the mistake of letting go my old footman, in favor of someone younger and stronger." The embers of his cigar glowed an angry red, with a large intake of breath. "I must have been a simpleton to assume that such a young beauty like Charlotte would remain loyal to an old man like me."

"What are you getting at, man?" Langsdale commanded.

Lord Hastings chuckled – a deep, dark chuckle that set Langsdale on edge. The burly man blew one last cloud of smoke before crushing his cigar into a crystal ashtray on the console table he stood beside. Then, he proceeded toward Langsdale with slow, methodical steps. He came to a stop at the inspector's side, dark eyes heavily considering the gruesome face on the wall.

"Such a fine piece, this. One of a kind, in fact. A tough hunt, but worth the trouble in the end." He shook his head, clicking his tongue.

Langsdale stared at his large companion, the musky taste of second-hand cigar smoke ashing his mouth.

"A hunt?"

After a heavily pregnant pause, Hastings turned those dark, calculating eyes on Langsdale. His expression abruptly made sense of the man who'd run for his life the previous night.

"It was a well-deserved and rewarding victory – against one younger and stronger."

Horror sank Langsdale's stomach. A tremor took up in his knees, turning them to jelly as his gaze returned to the lifeless, gaping visage above their heads. The gas lamp's flickering light cast the face in eerie shadow, mouth and empty eyes seeming to stretch and contract in what Langsdale was now realizing was a petrified scream of terror.

"My God," he gasped, whirling on his companion. But he was too late; a pistol from the opposite pocket of Hasting's dressing gown was drawn, taking deadly aim upon Langsdale's chest. A wicked grin spread his lips, like the horrible smiling masks around the room.

"I must say, I do not yet have the mask of a police inspector from Scotland Yard. It will make a fine addition to my trinkets."

GREED HATH NO PLACE

Originally published by Timber Ghost Press (2022)

I wasn't about to let myself suffer.

Nature hadn't been kind to Ellsworth County that year, but most especially not to me. A wicked blizzard ripped through us the beginning of winter, laying waste to an already devastated community. Summer storms that always swept across central Kansas never came, leaving tilled soil to crack and dehydrate in the harsh sun. Seedling crops spoiled in the sweltering heat, leaving us no food to survive on. No choice but to hunker down and prepare for a rough end to the year.

"We'll have to start rationing food," Dale told me. "What little we got from the crops can go around for a few days, but until the church sends emergency assistance we need to come together and share our resources." He took my hands, squeezing them. Smiling weakly. "The Lord will see us through this, Rose. I promise."

I quietly nodded, though I had to bite my tongue. My husband always cared for the town more than he did for me, and it showed. He was always doing more for them, giving them the shirt off his back – and mine too, without ever asking if I agreed. And he got all the praise for it. "Oh, Pastor Gresham, thank you," the sheep bleated, laying themselves at his feet. Always begging for more. And when everything in Ellsworth went to waste, he bore the brunt of everyone else's suffering first.

I was left to suffer on my own yet again.

So naturally, when the first signs of a fledgling miracle came to pass, I took things into my own hands. Literally. I found a vine growing in my withered garden, poking up from the ice-crusted earth. Thick and green, standing out against the dark vegetation buried by snow. It wove through the entirety of the plot, bearing juicy red berries from delicate pink blossoms. There were hundreds, more than enough to see the town through until help arrived.

But if it was an act of God, then he must have finally heard my prayers. I bent to pluck the vine, to squirrel it away before Dale could find it. Could share it among the undeserving. The vine shuddered with each pull, shaking snow from its speckled leaves. Rustling up from death, like a snake in the grass. It was nearly free when something sharp jabbed into my finger.

"Shit." The vine came free, and I turned it over to look. The sharp end of a thorn had punctured my finger, but hadn't drawn any blood. The skin only reddened around the puncture hole, numbing the nerves from shock. I shook the thorn loose, rubbing my finger against my thumb. Perhaps the berries weren't the answer to my prayers after all – but God no longer had a say in that. I took the vine into the house, cutting the berries loose and washing them. Storing them in glass jars that I hid beneath the floorboards in the den. Should my husband decide our hunger wasn't above the piss-poor of this filthy town, he'd be on his own.

The numbness from the thorn still hadn't left my finger by the time Dale came home. I did my best to hide the redness and irritation, ignoring the pins and needles as I served him a small dinner of greens left over from the pantry.

"The situation is getting worse. I still haven't heard from the deacon if help is coming." He pushed the plate of food away. "I don't feel right eating, while so many others are starving."

No thanks. No consideration for my efforts or my feelings. As always.

That night, I didn't sleep. I couldn't. The numbness had thankfully abated, but a new problem had risen: guilt. I kept thinking of those damn berries, sitting beneath our floorboards. Safely tucked away where no one would ever find them. I was up and down all night, pacing the bedroom while my husband peacefully slept through his stomach's growling hunger. It caused my own stomach to turn, ablaze with fiery indigestion. I went to the bathroom, splashed cold water onto my face. Gazed at myself in the mirror. I looked puffy and irritated.

"Get over it," I whispered, before shutting off the light and forcing myself back into bed. "Finders keepers."

But the guilt kept growing. I found myself unable to get out of bed the next day, from how heavy it had gotten. Or perhaps because of how heavy I'd gotten. Overnight, my entire body had swelled, skin tender and tingling. Radiating from the thorn prick on my finger. Dale didn't seem to notice; he'd gotten up before me, preparing for sermon. Only coming to check if I was getting out of bed for church.

"I don't feel well. I'm going to sleep in today."

"I'm sorry, Rose. I'll be out for a while; I'm coordinating the division of what food we have left after service today." He kissed my forehead, placing something on my nightstand. "Here's a copy of the sermon, in case you feel well enough to read it."

When he'd left, I managed to roll over and grab the notecard. Promptly ripping it up.

The Good Lord will always provide. Greed hath no place among the righteous.

I finally managed to force myself up before noon, but it was difficult. I felt made of cement, stiff and heavy. Barely able to move. It took all the effort I could muster to drag myself out of bed, to carry the weight of my body on legs that refused to bend. To turn on the lights and head downstairs, refusing to face myself in the mirror. Terrified of what I would see.

By the time I made it to the den, I had swelled even more. Something inside my bulging stomach sloshed with every step, rolling back and forth like marbles. Drawing nausea to my chest every time. I glanced at the thorn prick on my finger. It was red and angry, puckered into puffy flesh. The recliner creaked beneath my body, which was growing ever heavier. Ever bigger. Had I just left the vine alone, this wouldn't have happened.

I was just so tired of sharing. Of giving and giving and giving, never once receiving.

I'm glad Dale didn't come home right away. It would have been hard for him to see. To realize how truly selfish his wife had been beneath it all. I managed to open the floorboards before I could no longer move, confined to the recliner as my body ballooned out of control. Sloshing as it grew full of marbles. They came up my throat, spilling out of my mouth – berries from the vine. Producing more than enough berries to feed Ellsworth for weeks. Suffocating me, just as much as my guilt. Thankfully, Dale had left the letter opener close enough on the side table for me to reach. A quick jab was all it took, just like the thorn on the vine.

I wasn't about to let myself suffer anymore.

THE SCREAMING LADY OF PITCH ROAD

"You might want to slow down."

Billy finally pulled his face from his bag, licking rubbery lips. Chocolate dribbled and smeared across the fake vampire fangs still in his mouth, causing Vicki to cringe. "Why?" he asked around a mouthful of something gummy, blue eyes wide and inquiring. "It's my candy."

"Well, two things'll happen." Vicki held up two mummy-cloth wrapped fingers. "One, you'll have a wicked stomachache. And two, you won't have any left over to trade at school." She raised an eyebrow. "What do you think about that?"

Concern shaded Billy's brow, heavier than the shadow that hung between street lamps as Halloween curfew approached. They sidestepped a pack of giggling children, also ravenously digging through their candy bags. Billy glanced at them before returning his gaze to Vicki. "But I don't want to trade."

"Did you miss the part about the stomachache?"

"Can't I just have one more piece?"

Vicki sighed, rolling her eyes. She snatched the heavy bag from Billy's hands, slinging it over her shoulder. "Absolutely not."

"Aw, c'mon, Vicki!" His high-pitched whine echoed around the street. Thankfully, it was starting to empty out; only a few stragglers slunk from house to house, playing their last round of trick or treat that year. "That's not fair! Give it back!"

"No." Vicki hoisted it higher, away from his grubby little reach. "We're already late coming home tonight, and Mom would kill me if I let you get yourself sick on top of it all."

Billy stomped to a halt beneath a flickering street lamp, crossing his arms in a huff. Badly painted brows knitted together. "You're mean, Vicki."

Vicki turned. "No I'm not. I'm trying to keep both of us out of trouble." She reached for his arm. "Now c'mon, we have to get going. I don't want to have to go down Pitch Road to get home if we can help it."

Billy shrugged off her grasp, stubbornly shaking his head. When she tried again, his eyes fell to the ground, nose wrinkling. A sniffle echoed across the now empty street. Not ready to hear her mother's complaints about a sad little brother on top of everything else, Sam closed her eyes and took a deep breath. She tossed her head back, opening her eyes to the star-blanketed sky.

"Look, Billy." She laid the lumpy candy bag on the ground, sinking to one knee. "You have to see things from my point of view. I'm your big sister, and you are my responsibility. You always will be, even when we're grown up. Sometimes, making sure that you're not going to hurt yourself sounds like I'm being mean." Vicki waited until Billy's tear-filled eyes finally met hers. She offered him a smile. "But it's just because I love you and I'm trying to protect you, kiddo."

Billy stared for a moment, frown beginning to loosen.

"You mean it?"

"Of course I mean it." Vicki stood, taking the bag of candy with her. Her grin widened as she reached in, pulling out a single Snickers - Billy's favorite candy. "Now, if you promise to be good and we're able to get home without having to take Pitch Road, you can have just one last piece."

Billy's eyes lit up. He nodded eagerly, all traces of sorrow gone from his face.

"I promise!"

Vicki giggled as he snatched the treat from her palm, tearing open the wrapping and popping the square of chocolate into his mouth. Then he hugged her leg.

"I love you, Vic."

Slinging the bag over her shoulder once more, she took Billy's hand. Together, they walked down the street in the direction of home.

"I love you too, Billy."

***

By the time the siblings had reached the end of the neighborhood, it was nearly curfew. One by one, orange and purple lights lining the houses began to flicker out, leaving the yellowish street lamps as their only source of light. Vicki felt her heart begin to drop. The safest way home was by the main road, which was well-lit by street lamps. But the quickest way was a narrow dirt road that branched off nearby, weaving through the woods that separated their neighborhood on Harrison Street from Platte Lane, which they were currently on. It would cut their travel time by half, if not more.

But Pitch Road was supposedly where the screaming lady was.

She'd heard the tale a few times since starting middle school that year. Those who walked alone on Pitch Road, at any time of the day, were at risk of running into the screaming ghost of the woman that haunted the woods. According to the hushed whispers in class, the woman had been taking the Pitch Road shortcut when she was hit by an oncoming car. She would appear to those who were about to be hit, too. The story was enough to scare the socks off of anyone - true or not. No one at school had ever seen her and it was very rare for a car to drive down Pitch Road, which led Vicki to be skeptical.

But as they came to the entrance of Pitch Road, Vicki stopped to consider the shadowy path.

"What's wrong, Vic?" Billy asked.

Vicki pulled her phone from her pocket, glancing at the time. "Curfew is in ten minutes. If we aren't home by then, Mom will skin us alive." She tucked it away, chewing her lower lip. "The main road takes fifteen minutes to walk." A heavy swallow galloped down her throat. She nodded to the dirt path. "But if we take Pitch Road, we'll be home in five."

Billy stuck out his lower lip, suddenly looking nervous. He shifted closer to Vicki's legs. "Do we have to?"

Vicki put on the bravest face she could. "It's better than getting scolded, isn't it?"

"Uh-uh." Billy shook his head. "I don't want to see the screaming lady."

"I don't either, but we don't really have a choice." The longer she stared the darkness seemed to come alive, Pitch Road writhing into its deep maw like a serpent. "We have to get home. Besides, it's curfew, so there won't be any cars on the road. So we should be just fine."

"I'm scared," Billy whimpered.

Vicki took his hand, squeezing it tight. "Don't worry, kiddo. The screaming lady probably isn't even real. It's probably just a story people started telling to keep people off the road." She set her jaw grimly, pulling out her phone once again. She activated the flashlight feature; a swath of intense light illuminated the path ahead of them, piercing the outer layer of darkness. "And if we hurry, it won't seem as bad."

Once they were on Pitch Road, keeping as close to the center as possible, Vicki's brief spurt of courage began to fade. The flashlight barely penetrated the darkness between gnarled tree trunks, elongating their shadows into ghastly figures reflected on the shrubbery beyond. Wind whistled through bare branches above them. Billy squeezed Vicki's hand so tight it began to throb.

"What's that?" he whispered, shivering.

"It's only the wind," Vicki replied, trying to keep her voice even. She gestured upward with a nod of her head. "When it blows through the branches, it sounds like that."

"It sounds like screaming."

"I know it does." Vicki refocused on the road, holding her phone up higher. "But it's not the screaming lady. I promise."

"How do you know?" Billy demanded, stopping short, wide eyes darting all directions.

Vicki sighed. "You know how when you swing a branch around it makes a whoosh sound?" When Billy nodded, Vicki spread her hands. "It's the same thing. The branches are just…whooshing." As if punctuating her statement, the breeze ripped through the trees again. "See?"

Billy shook his head, biting his lower lip. "That's not whooshing, Vicki."

Vicki paused to listen, realizing that Billy was right. Something else struck up with the breeze, high-pitched and fierce. Something that sounded like a terrified scream, rising on the wind close behind them.

"VICKI!"

Vicki gasped and whirled on her heel, shining her flashlight the direction they'd come from. It reflected off a glowing figure, ethereal and white, standing in the middle of the dirt road where they'd walked only moments ago. Vicki threw an arm up, protecting her eyes from the light. Once her vision adjusted she realized the figure was a young woman, arms outstretched and mouth open wide in a terrified scream. Another moment longer, and Vicki finally realized that the blinding light was not coming from the woman, but from a truck speeding up the road behind her.

Without hesitation, Vicki grabbed Billy's upper arm and dove sideways. She wrapped her arms around him, holding tight as they rolled into the shrubs - narrowly missing the bumper of a truck full of laughing, oblivious teenagers. Pebbles and twigs pelted them as the truck roared by, disappearing into the darkness down the rest of Pitch Road.

Vicki waited until silence had settled before loosening her grip on her little brother. She flopped onto her back in the grass, breathing hard. Staring up at the stars that peppered the sky between the branches. Once her heart rate came under control, she turned to Billy and found him sitting up, staring at the road in shock.

"Billy...you okay?"

He nodded, but didn't reply. Following his gaze, Vicki found the ghostly woman still standing in the road. She smiled happily, hands clasped at her waist and long hair rippling softly.

"The screaming lady…she saved us," Billy said softly.

"Yeah. I guess she did." Vicki sat up, brushing dirt and leaves from her clothes. She untangled the mummy cloth from her arms, which was caught up in the shrubbery behind her. However, she kept her eyes on the woman. "I wonder why."

"Maybe she didn't want to see us hurt." Billy finally peeled his eyes from the dirt road, looking at Vicki. "Maybe she wanted to give us a chance…like the chance she didn't have."

Vicki swallowed, glancing back to their silent spectator. "Uh…th-thank you. I guess."

The woman smiled wider, dipping her head in acknowledgement. Then she faded into thin air, leaving nothing behind but a quiet breeze whispering through the trees. Somehow, Pitch Road suddenly didn't seem as dark or scary. Vicki got to her feet and pulled Billy to his.

"C'mon…let's get out of here."

Before Vicki could react, Billy flung his arms around her legs and hugged her tight.

"Thank you, Vicki."

"For what?"

"You were right – you weren't being mean. You protected me, just like you said."

Vicki couldn't help but grin. "I told you so, kiddo." After peeling him from her leg, she picked up the candy bag and reached inside. Another Snickers appeared between her fingers, which she handed to her very happy little brother. "Screaming lady or not, I'll always be there for you. Even when we're grown up."

THIS WAY TO THE GOATMAN

*Originally published in The Vanishing Point Magazine, Issue *1 (2021)*

"Are you sure this is safe?"

Kendra struck a match, its actinic flare casting shadows that deepened her annoyed frown. She ignored the question, touching the flame to the wick of the black pillar candle before her.

"Its fine, Lucas. This bridge has been here since the 1800's. The worst that can happen is we get splinters and bit by mosquitos."

Lucas swallowed down the plethora of concerns in his throat, watching her methodically shake out the match. Striking a new one, touching it to the next candle. Then the next. The flickering light grew with each lit wick, until they were surrounded by a circle of warmth. It weakly illuminated the graffiti-covered iron trusses to either side, attracting a swarm of curious insects from the stretch of woodland beyond the bridge's crossing. A chill raced down Lucas's spine.

"I meant the ritual."

A heavy sigh blew from Kendra's nose. She hoisted herself to her feet, grabbing the canister of table salt she'd stolen from the kitchen. It cascaded from the spout, drawing a line of white outside the ring of candles encompassing them.

"It's fine. I Googled it."

"Are you sure—"

The salt hissed to a stop, leaving the circle partly open near Lucas's side. She shot a glare over her shoulder, brown eyes flashing dangerously in the dancing flames.

"Do you want to sit in the truck, then?" She gestured angrily to the opening in the salt circle. "If so, this is your last chance. Once I close the circle, we're stuck. Nothing can come in or out unless permission is granted."

Lucas stared, unsure of what to do. He considered the gap closely, chewing on his lower lip. Eyes falling across the silhouetted treetops, from which came a grating cacophony of insectile shrieking. He should leave, knowing what they were getting themselves into. Despite a history of unexplained occurrences and police reports, their parents had tried their best to discredit the 'nonsense' about the supposed demon of the woods – the Goatman. It was only a myth, they said, invented to keep people from doing stupid things and getting themselves hurt. There was no such thing as a half-man, half-goat that haunted Old Alton Bridge.

But that explanation didn't sit well with everyone else living in Copper Canyon. From what Kendra told him, she'd been cornered in the locker room after declaring she didn't believe in the Goatman. She'd been tormented for daring to speak ill of him, for trying to explain the inexplicable. Dared to prove for herself if the Goatman was real or not. She'd come home like a storm cloud – agitated, brooding, and black and blue. Thundering up the stairs before their parents could see and locking herself in her room. Ignoring Lucas's pleas to go trick or treating. When she'd finally reappeared, cleaned up and bandaged, she demanded Lucas take a ride with her.

And here they wound up, sitting in the middle of Goatman's Bridge at midnight on Halloween, in the middle of an abandoned forest. Building a ritual circle. Attempting to summon the demon of the woods.

"I don't think we should be doing this. What if someone catches us?"

"It's Halloween night – no one's out here. The Goatman isn't real." Kendra's eyes narrowed. "And I'm going to prove it to everyone once and for all." She turned back to the gap in the salt circle, tipping the canister. Letting salt waterfall down, closing them in with a complete, solid white line.

A hush fell over the woods – though it could have been because the time-eaten planks rattled beneath the canister as Kendra set it down. The cloud of insects around their candles dispersed, lingering just outside the ring of light. Looping in slow, methodical figures. She settled on the opposite side of the circle, hand reaching for the backpack she brought along. Setting it in her lap and unzipping it. From within she pulled out a flat, rectangular board and set it face-up on the splintered wood between them. Lucas swallowed hard.

"A spirit board?"

"The veil between worlds is supposedly at its thinnest right now. It's the only way to contact a demon, if they actually exist." She retrieved the board's planchette from the bottom of the bag, placing it atop the curved letters and numbers across its shadowy face. Lastly, she held out a compact notebook and pen. "I need you to take notes of what the board says."

Lucas nervously accepted the items, trying not to tremble as Kendra touched the tips of her fingers to the curved bottom of the planchette. Her pink tongue poked between her lips in concentration.

"Are there any spirits with us on this bridge tonight?" She began, voice cutting through the muted hush. A faint echo repeated back, thrumming between the rusted iron trusses. Lucas's already pounding heart skipped a few beats.

"C'mon, Kendra, we should leave…"

"I already told you we can't," she cut him off with a scathing glare. "If you were gonna be chicken shit about it, you should have said something earlier."

"You didn't say we were going to Goatman's Bridge!" He squeaked.

Kendra's lips peeled back into an angry snarl. "Of all the people to have my back, it should be you! You know the whole Goatman thing is bullshit!"

Lucas shoved the notebook off his lap, letting it fall to the planks. The candle flames flickered as he shakily got to his knees. "If you don't believe any of this is real, then why can't we just break the circle and go home?"

"Fine. Go home, then." The sounds of the woods died to near silence at her clipped command. Her eyes smoldered, honey embers in the candlelight. Jaw flexing in pinched anger. "See for yourself what happens when you tell Mom and Dad what we've been doing instead of trick or treating."

A heavy lump swelled in the back of Lucas's throat. Fear greater than that of the Goatman forced him back into his seat. Dutifully taking the notebook back into his lap. Clearing her throat, Kendra refocused her attention on the board.

"Are there any spirits with us on the bridge tonight?"

The silence continued, leaving them with only flickering shadows. The burbling creek that snaked below the bridge, once blotted out by the insects, rushed like rapids in the pressing quiet. After a long pause, Lucas dared to look up. Kendra remained focused on the spirit board, chestnut curls framing her face – bringing out the sharpest angles of her hawkish features.

Then her hands began to move. His eyes widened as the planchette scraped across the board in long, elaborate loops.

"Are you doing that?" He asked nervously.

"No." Kendra's eyes followed the planchette as it slowed, coming to rest on the word in the upper left corner.

Yes.

"Yes, there's a spirit here?"

The planchette didn't move. Lucas stared at it, watching it quiver beneath Kendra's fingertips, poised like a tiger ready to pounce. The candles sputtered between rapid breaths issuing from her lips. Eyes narrowed, she leaned forward. Staring into the glass eye of the planchette.

"What the hell..." she whispered faintly.

"What is it?" Lucas hissed, leaning forward to see.

Kendra's hands came up, a shriek piercing the silence of the night. Lucas's heart leapt into his throat, choking in a fit of startled coughing. His vision tunneled, adrenaline thrusting his gut into a wave of nausea. He managed to gasp his way out of unconsciousness, only to realize that his sister was giggling.

"That's not funny, Kendra!"

"Of course it's funny," she wiped a tear from her eye, stifling laughter behind her hand. "And of course I was moving it the whole time. This shit isn't real, Lucas. And I just proved it to you." She spread her hands to encompass the darkness. The silence that pressed in on all sides. "There's no such thing as the Goatman."

Clickety clack, clickety clack.

The creaking planks drew a real scream from Kendra's throat this time. A jolt of fright caused her knee to bump the spirit board, shifting the planchette across its face. Lucas caught sight of motion behind her head; a dark figure approached, silhouette barely visible against the moonless backdrop of night. Kendra followed his gaze, whipping over her shoulder. Gasping at the shadow that loomed ever closer.

"Who's there?" she screeched.

The figure slowed as it stepped into the yellowed candle light. A man looked back at them, dark skin glowing warm in the suffused light. His eyes were dim beneath an old-fashioned straw hat, wrinkled at the corners in weathered crow's feet. He sported a gnarled wooden cane that tapped against the planks as he walked.

"Here now, what's goin' on?" His voice was gentle but booming. Friendly. He looked at Kendra and Lucas in turn. "What're you two doin' out here on a night like this? Shouldn't y'all be at home?"

It took a moment for both to recover from shock. "Uh," Kendra eventually blurted, a hot blush burning pink across her cheeks. "I-I...we..."

The old man glanced at the spirit board, the black candles. At Kendra and Lucas's petrified faces. Then his eyes fell on the salt circle; a smirk tugged one side of his thin lips. Something about it riddled Lucas's chest with anxiety. "Lemme guess – ya'll are trying to make contact with the Goatman, ain't ya?"

"Y-yeah," Kendra sounded mortified.

"I seen many kids like you come out here, tryin' the same thing before. Over'n over'n over again. Ain't nothin' come through for them, o'course." He leaned atop the cane, pointing a gnarled finger at the spirit board. "'Course, ain't none of them had a spirit board, neither."

Lucas glanced at the abandoned planchette. At how, despite Kendra's startled motion as the old man approached, it remained over the word Yes.

"Wh-what are you doing out here this time of night?" Lucas forced himself to ask.

"Me? I live 'round here." The old man pointed over his shoulder, back toward the darkness he came from. "Right up there, just past the bridge. Ain't nobody usually out here at night, so I come a'walkin' for peace o'mind." A deep chuckled welled up from his chest. "Well, 'course that's different tonight, bein' All Hallows Eve." He nodded to their circle. To the board. "Y'all had any luck with that thing?"

"No," Kendra replied quietly, shaking her head. "It's fake…demons aren't real."

"Well, now, I wouldn't say that." The old man pursed his lips. "There's a lot o'things in this world that can't never be explained. I lived a long time, and to this day I still ain't sure of some'o the things I seen out in these woods. Some'o the things I heard."

"What things?"

"There's sure some demons in these here woods – not just the Goatman, neither." The old man scratched his chin, fingertips scraping against wiry stubble. "I seen many a'wanderin' travelers go into these here woods, havin' yet to come back. Searchin' for somethin' they ain't got no business tryin' to contact. Y'can sometimes hear 'em up and down these trails, hollerin' and crashin' 'round. Wantin' to make themselves heard. To be found. They's the ones that're easy to steer clear of. But the others…" His eyes went dark. "The ones ya can't see'n hear are the most dangerous of 'em all. The ones that sneak up on ya, in the dead o'night, with ain't a whisper o'warnin'. One second you're alone, then in the next, they jump ya."

Ice settled in the pit of Lucas's stomach. He glanced at Kendra, whose eyes were wide and nervous. Fixated on the old man. After a long moment of uncomfortable silence, his dark gaze met hers. The smile returned to his wizened lips.

"Y'all ever even used a spirit board before now?"

"N-no." Kendra managed to sputter.

The smile widened, showing nearly all of his yellowed, grimy teeth. "I can show ya how, if ya like."

Lucas cut off Kendra's reply before she could make it – if she even had one. "Where did you say you lived again?" he shakily demanded, clenching trembling fists.

The old man's eyes met his, narrowing. That wide, creepy smile remained frozen to his face. "My apologies, I didn't introduce myself proper-like." A hand fanned across his chest. "The name's Oscar. I live just up north beyond the bridge, like I told ya. Down the path and into the woods a little. I own a farm up thataway. Just a little goat farm, that's all." He stuck a thumb over his shoulder. "Didn't ya see the sign before ya crossed the bridge?"

The siblings shook their heads. Oscar chuckled again. "It's a little hard to see in the dark – 'specially since y'all didn't have yer headlights on."

"How did you know we didn't have our headlights on?" Kendra asked suspiciously.

"Once ya live alone in a place for so long, ya learn to be a little wary of yer surroundin's." He touched the brim of his straw hat with his thumb, pushing it further up above his eyes. He leaned heavily on his cane again. "I only been caught once unawares by someone crossin' without no headlights. And that was enough fer me." His eyes fell back to the spirit board. "Now, how 'bout that spirit board?"

"It doesn't work," Lucas piped up, starting to get scared. "Demons aren't real, like my sister says."

Oscar slowly shook his head. His smile never faded. "Still ain't convinced, is ya?" He rapped the bottom of his cane against the bridge's wooden planks. They rattled in their casings. "Listen. I ain't just some fuddy-duddy what lives by himself in the woods. I ain't got no reason to make up fairytales 'bout the things I seen." He pointed to the spirit board again. "I used one o'them many times before, and I guarantee y'all are missin' the key to makin' it work."

"What would that be?" Kendra demanded, beginning to sound like her old self again – annoyed.

"An open mind." Those dark eyes met hers once more. "Let me show ya how to use it. If it ain't gonna work, then you got solid proof that demons are fake. Ain't that right?"

"Yeah, I guess so."

"That's right." Oscar's cane swirled as his hands opened, taking in the salt circle. "Now, may I join y'all?"

"Yeah."

Oscar didn't move right away. Kendra frowned up at him. "Well, what are you waiting for?"

The old man's smile tightened wickedly. "'Course y'know, it ain't proper to allow someone into yer circle without permission. Ya gotta clear a path fer me, that's all."

Every hair on the back of Lucas's neck stood rigid. But before he could protest, Kendra shrugged. Reaching forward, she swept away part of the salt circle – at the toes of Oscar's worn, holey leather boots.

The shrieking of the cicadas and crickets returned, rising up in a swell of thunder. The insects swarming the candlelight evaporated from the bridge in a startled flutter. Lucas's heart dropped into his stomach as Oscar set his cane down and stepped across the salt line, lowering himself to the planks with crossed legs. The candle flames hissed and spat, sending hot black wax dripping across the wood. Oscar didn't seem to notice the wax that rolled onto the cuffs of his trouser legs; he kept his eyes on the spirit board, kept the grin plastered to his weathered face.

"Now, put yer fingertips on that there planchette again," he breathed heavily.

Kendra looked wary, but did as she was told. Her fingertips touched the rounded edges of the planchette, bringing it back to the center of the board.

"Ask yer question."

"Are there any spirits on the bridge with us—" Kendra barely got the words out before her hands began flying across the board in long, circular motions. She drew a ragged, terrified gasp. Lucas bit his lower lips so hard he tasted blood. Oscar didn't move at all.

"Stop doing that, Kendra!" he demanded shakily. "I told you it's not funny!"

"It's not me, I swear!" she cried, tears welling up in her eyes. They dripped onto the edge of the board as the planchette stopped, then jerked her hands forward and up – to the top left corner.

Yes.

"What is this?" Kendra sobbed. Her gaze flew up to Oscar, who sat perfectly still beside them. Dark eyes wide open and focused on the planchette. The grin began to eat his entire face as Kendra's hands were dragged along the board like a rag doll's. "How are you doing that?"

"I told you, there's demons in these here woods." The wicked smile turned on Kendra. Oscar's eyes glowed a diffuse, honey gold as the candle flames grew into hot, sputtering fires. "You just ain't listenin'. No one listens, 'specially when they's crossed into my territory."

"Who are they?" She pleaded. "Who are the demons?"

The planchette tore across the board. Dragging Kendra's arms along in three, quick jerks.

YOU

The ring of flames blew out in a gust of wind. Kendra's scream was silenced in a choked-off, bloody gurgle. Something large and powerful clipped Lucas's left side before he could react, knocking him back across the rotting planks of wood. The back of his head hit a candle, hot wax searing his scalp and clinging to his hair. Panicking, he flipped onto his stomach and pushed himself to hands and knees. Splinters jabbed into his palms as he shoved himself upward, screaming. Running for the truck parked at the entrance of the bridge. He grabbed the door handle and yanked, but it was locked. He slammed a fist against the window, willing it to open. Trying to ignore the scuffling behind him. Too late, the thought crossed his mind that he needed the keys to get in – finally registering that he'd left Kendra behind. Lucas whirled.

"Kendra!"

A large, dark blot squirmed in the center of the bridge. Heavy, wet squelching added staccato to the insects echoing Lucas's panic. To the planks of the bridge, which creaked and rattled as the inky blot began to take a shape. It rose on two legs, darker than black, outlined against the moonless night. The straw hat on its head fell away, exposing two thick, short horns that ended in sharp, dagger-like points. Dripping with clots of blood.

"What are you?" Lucas wailed tearfully.

The shape slowly turned. Two, piercing yellow eyes burned like flames in the dark, staring straight ahead. A golden lining to a short snout protruding from an inhuman face. The low growl that emanated from its throat ended in a chuckle, vibrating through the iron trusses in Oscar's voice.

"Didn't ya see the sign, boy?"

The right arm rose, toward the bridge's structure. Lucas followed its direction, to a rust-bitten tin sign hammered into the truss. A sign they hadn't seen when he and Kendra pulled up in the truck with their headlights off, armed only with candles and reckless stupidity. Lucas barely caught its time-rubbed words before the shape pounced, goring his throat with the horns atop its head. Spilling fresh, hot blood across the planks of Old Alton Bridge.

This way to the Goatman.

FROM THE GROUND UP

Originally published in "Earth: Element Cycle Book One" by Eerie River Publishing (2022)

The scream came from somewhere to the northeast, ricocheting off the craggy ridgeline. Startled crows mimicked the blood-curdling screech, fleeing between the decaying pines. A spray of crisp needles rained down, cutting through the mist clinging to the branches. They pattered against Samantha's campaign brim, pin-pricking dark spots into her flashlight's halo. She froze, ears pricked. Sweeping her beam across the fog.

"I am a Malheur National Forest park ranger," she called again, slowly and clearly. "If you can hear me, please respond. I am trying to locate your position."

Hushed warbling returned to the underbrush, from insects that sounded just as uncertain as she felt. Samantha did her best to swallow it down, cautiously overstepping a felled trunk. Boots squelching into the spongy earth. She was very familiar with the Clear Creek trail that crossed the

Prairie City District of the Strawberry Mountains, but she had never wandered this far off the path. She never had to; the path was wide and clearly marked, parallel to the creek that weaved along the face of the slopes. Even inexperienced hikers knew to stay on the clear side of the ridgeline – so the desperate cries she'd heard from the outpost had come as a complete shock.

Something snapped, crackling about the misty graveyard of gnarled trunks. Samantha brought her flashlight up, squinting. Searching the dusky shadows. Cursing herself for having gone out alone. "Hello?"

"Sam."

Samantha whirled, feet slipping in the slick soil. Foul-smelling mud sprayed upward as she hit the ground, coating her arms and face. The flashlight escaped her fingers, rolling away. Illuminating a portly figure looming behind a tree.

"Randy!" She rolled onto her belly, pushing herself to her knees. Mud spread between her fingertips, cold and gelatinous. She grimaced, swatting it off against her pants. "Oh my god. Don't sneak up on me like that!"

"Sorry."

Samantha snatched the flashlight up, shaking her head. Sizing up her outpost partner with a mixture of relief and frustration. "Where the hell have you been? You've been gone for days."

The burly ranger stepped forward, fog swirling about his shoulders. His eyes were shaded by his cap, hooded against the harsh yellow light. "Sorry," he repeated flatly, spreading his meaty hands. "I didn't mean to leave you alone. I had something I had to do."

Samantha turned back to the woods. "Well, in case you didn't hear it, someone was screaming from the trail. There haven't been any hikers up Clear Creek today as far as I know, so whoever it is must have come up shortly before my shift started." She gestured forward. "The last time I heard anything was right before you showed up. Beyond those trees." Her skin prickled; the remnants of viscous mud were cold, starting to itch. She did her best to ignore it. "How could they have been stupid enough to veer off the path?"

"Maybe they were looking for something?" Randy suggested, although he didn't sound convinced. His gaze remained fixed on her.

"Maybe." She looked upward, to the canopy of bare branches crisscrossed above. "But it's almost impossible to see through this fog." Samantha shook her head. "No, that doesn't make sense. What would make them cross the creek, especially at sundown? There's nothing out here."

"I am here."

The faint voice drew Samantha back around, flashlight rising. It finally seemed to penetrate the dense gloom, revealing a narrow path snaked between a cluster of jagged trees, jutting up like the fingers of a clutching hand. Their roots were exposed, covered by wide, flat mushrooms and veiny fungus.

"Hello! We hear you! We're park rangers, we're here to help you!"

"Let's go look," Randy said softly.

Samantha picked her way forward, careful to avoid stepping into any more slick spots. Twigs and dry vines snapped beneath her boots, echoing into the endless dim. Finally, there was movement ahead; the fog swirled in the center of the decrepit little grove, around the shoulders of a dark shape with its arms raised. Flagging her down.

"Don't move, I see you!" Her pace quickened. She trampled a patch of honey-colored fungi as she squeezed between the close-knit trunks. The scent of bitter, earthy mold grew strong as Samantha entered the ring of trees, sweeping the flashlight back and forth. Finding nothing but an empty clearing.

"Where are you?" Samantha spun, frantically searching the darkness, shining light into the gaping holes of rot burrowed into the trees. The one closest to her - a bulbous, stocky trunk barely taller than herself - was filled with sickly white and yellow fungus. It clung to the rims, to the insides. Oozing pale liquid in thick globs down the bark. "Where did you go?"

"*I am here.*" The voice whispered from all directions. Through the trees, from the mud; from within her own head.

"Where?" Samantha found herself facing the way she had come. The tree trunks seemed closer together, narrowing the gap she had somehow managed to squeeze through. Obscured by a heavy fog that hadn't been there before. It was only then she noticed Randy had not followed her. She stood on tip-toe, peering through the fork in the stunted tree. Seeing nothing. "Randy? Randy, where are you?"

"*Everywhere.*"

Samantha's skin crawled. She settled back on her heels, turning. Staring at the infestation overtaking the bark. A chagrined scoff escaped her lips. "Real fucking cute. First it was the whole lost, terrified hiker shtick, and now you're pulling a disappearing act on me?" She shrugged, arms slapping against her hips. Causing the skin beneath the slippery mud to itch worse. "No wonder our outpost is the damn laughing stock of the district."

"*Turn off the light*," the soft voice returned – now very clearly Randy's voice, "*and you will see me.*"

"I'm not in the mood for games."

"*Turn off the light.*"

Heaving a frustrated sigh, Samantha extinguished the flashlight and tucked it into her belt. Shadow and mist blinded her, sticking to her in droplets. Tickling her skin. Finally giving in, Samantha picked at the blotchy mud. It was oily and thick, the consistency of mucous. She grimaced. "Okay, the light's off. Happy now?"

"*Can you see me?*"

"It's dark," she bit back, digging at her arms. The itch intensified. "My eyes haven't adjusted yet." Her fingertips slipped and slid. "Where are you?"

"*Everywhere.*"

"Stop with that shit already." The itching turned into burning. Samantha growled, scratching harder. The slippery mud dribbled down her arm, preventing her from reaching the skin. "I'm getting really sick of it."

"*Join me.*"

Fed up, Samantha yanked the flashlight from her belt and flicked it back on so she could see. Nothing had changed, and there was no sign of Randy. There was only the perpetual mist, serenaded by chirping insects. She sighed again, bringing a hand to her face – and gasping at the sight of blood oozing down her arm. Down both arms, thick and congealed. The ridge of a bone, smooth and white, bubbled up just beneath the liquefied surface.

"*Join me.*"

She dropped the flashlight, splattering another layer of gelatinous mud against her boots. The entirety of the narrow grove glowed in its soft light, glistening in the silken mist. Samantha's head swam, almost as much as the peeling trees that danced across her vision. They undulated like snakes, bending and twisting. Creaking and groaning as they wove what remained of their branches into webs of confusion. The dizziness dropped her to her knees, before the cavernous bulk of the short tree. The air tasted thick and cool; the world stopped for an abrupt moment of clarity, in which Samantha became acutely aware of her surroundings. Of the mushrooms and soupy mud, how they pulsated and writhed. How they spewed puffs of fog, adding to the confluence she had been wandering through in search of a terrified scream – a scream that erupted from her own chest.

"Join me."

Gnarled limbs wrapped about her waist, gently pulling her to her feet. Mud and ichor sloughed off her arms, slopping heavily to the forest floor. Leaving behind eaten-away bones. Pieces of her jaw followed suit, splashing to her chest as a vine-wrapped branch tucked itself beneath her chin. Another two grasping her bony nubs, raising them above her head. The innards of the tree writhed, belching fumes. Cowling the stunted trunk. A trunk that suddenly looked so very much like Randy.

"Join me."

***

Samantha Harding and Randy Young were reported missing from the Prairie City Ranger District over a week later. A search and rescue team of their peers were quickly cobbled together, combing the face of the Strawberry Mountains near the team's outpost station. Their names echoed across the Clear Creek trail, falling flat on deaf ground. Eventually, someone found a set of preserved footprints leading off the path, into a thick set of uncharted woods. Rangers entered the woods in pairs of two, searching high and low. Into every crevice and under every rock. From the ground up.

"I think they eloped."

"Bullshit." A pair of searchers bickered, crunching through the thickening woods. Approaching a patch of fog that clung to shrubbery and trees on the other side of the creek. "You really think someone like Sam Harding would settle for a tub of lard like that?"

"She could be attracted to fat guys, you don't know."

"Neither do you." They stepped over a fallen tree. "For all we know, she was running from him and he chased her into the woods."

"You think he killed her?"

"I don't know, he could have. Y'know how some guys can be – if the girl doesn't want him, then he won't let anyone else have her. He'll start stalking her, showing up at her house unexpectedly…all that stuff."

"I like my theory better."

Something snapped ahead. The rangers stopped in their tracks, squinting through the thick vapor. Both brandishing their flashlights, illuminating the outline of a decaying grove of trees a few feet away.

"Samantha? Randy? Are you out there?"

"*I am here.*" The whisper was faint, coming from the direction of the grove. Between the gnarled trunks, two shadowy figures stood within the fog. Arms raised to be seen.

"We see you. We're coming!"

As the pair of rescuers hurried forward, crushing honey-colored fungi underfoot, the mist rippled apart into a clear path.

"*Join us.*"

GOOD TO THE LAST DROP

Originally published in "Monsters A-Z: Aliens" by Raven and Drake Books (2022)

"Max, it's your turn to go upstairs."

Max barely heard the quiet request. He dug his thumbs into the controls, boosting his speed. Shooting ahead of the other kart racers, narrowly escaping a banana peel in the road. He was so close to crossing the finish line in first...just a few more turns and he'd take the trophy...

"Max!"

His thumb slipped, costing him a single second of deceleration – in which he was immediately overtaken. Whistles and bells began going off as the race was called in favor of another player.

"Ugh, Mom! I just lost the tournament because of you!" Max growled unhappily, tossing his console onto the table and crossing his arms in a huff.

"Well I'm sorry, but I need a can of beans for dinner." His mother chopped vegetables on the counter across the kitchen, tossing the bits into the boiling pot on the stove. "And it's your turn to go upstairs."

"Can't Dad go? He's probably just sitting on the couch watching football and drinking Coke."

Mom didn't stop chopping. "He went yesterday."

Max rolled his eyes, running a hand through his hair. "Can I play just one more race before I go up there? Please?"

Mom's knife slapped into the cutting board, going silent for a moment. She didn't turn her head. "I said to go upstairs. I need the beans before the vegetables get soft."

Max swallowed heavily. There was no argument to be had with her tone. He glanced toward the carpeted stairs leading up to the main floor of the house; blanketed by shadow, too far from the light source of the kitchen and den to reach.

"Do I have to?"

"Everyone has to, Max." Mom's tone softened a bit. "I know it's scary, but you'll be all right. Just make sure to wear your mask and focus on the beans." She finally turned, blue eyes narrowed. "And don't respond to them, no matter how tempting it might be."

With a resounding sigh, Max slid off his chair and headed for the stairs. He opened the coat closet, reaching to the top shelf for the black straps that snaked down from it. A gas mask fell into his hands; he pulled it over his face, adjusting it securely. Tying it down in the back with a double knot to be extra safe. They'd never tried to pull it off him before, but he wasn't taking any chances. Not when he had a Mario Kart tournament to come back to.

"Headed up, son?" Dad's voice came from the den.

Max turned; Dad was in the den right where he knew he'd be, the old tube TV flashing with a rerun of some Superbowl or another.

"Yeah," Max responded.

"Do me a favor – grab me another Coke?"

"You're addicted to that stuff, Nick," came his mother's annoyed voice from the kitchen.

"Better Coke than something else, Anna," Dad shouted back, rolling his eyes. After a moment, he turned back to Max. "Get one for me?"

"Sure."

"Thanks, kid." He turned back to the screen, cheering uproariously as the team he rooted for scored a touchdown, acting like the game was live. Downing his Coke and crushing the can with his bare hand.

Grabbing the flashlight from the closet, Max closed the door and trotted up the stairs. The further up he went, however, the stronger his sense of dread started to get. His pace slowed with each step until he reached the landing at the top. Facing the door, bolted shut by several heavy locks and chains, his heart began to race. He should have gotten used to it by now – he'd been upstairs a handful of times since he'd turned 13 last month – but it was still scary to think about what was behind the door.

Aliens.

No one really knew where they came from, or what they wanted. Their ships had come down from the sky almost two years ago, but they didn't rain destruction like the movies had predicted. Instead, they simply spread out across the globe, invading people's homes. Offering to give them everything they've always wanted; money, toys, cars. They didn't seem dangerous at all – until people started disappearing. Everyone who accepted the aliens' offers ended up going missing without a trace.

In response, the governments of every country forced people into hiding underground. They told the world that the aliens were using some kind of chemical to lure people onto their ships, and that gas masks were required for self-protection. And if anyone needed to come above-ground, they were not to speak to the aliens at all. No matter what they said.

"Just think about getting back to your game," Max muttered to himself, starting to undo the locks. "Winning the tournament…that's all that matters."

As the last lock slid open, Max pushed through the door and quickly shut it behind himself. He turned the bolt lock, then stood on tip-toes to reach the chain lock at the top of the door. Once it was securely in place, he took a deep, filtered breath and turned to face the dark, dusty kitchen. With trembling fingers, he clicked on the flashlight.

A group of aliens sat at the old kitchen table, playing what looked like some kind of card game. They turned to look, huge black eyes glittering in the light. Max's breath froze in his chest.

"Human!" The aliens leapt from the table, waddling over to him on their stubby little legs. Swarming about him like mice, staring up from waist-height with hopeful little smiles across the slits of their mouths. "Human, have you finally decided to accept our offer?"

Max swallowed, the beam of light trembling as his hands started to shake. He aimed it toward the pantry on the other side of the kitchen, taking a step forward. The aliens split, but remained close to his sides.

"Do you want to become a prince? We can make that happen!"

"All the candy in the galaxy can be yours if you come with us!"

"Do you want a puppy? I hear they are the best friends of humans!"

Just ignore them, Max repeated to himself in his head, biting his cheeks to keep his mouth shut. He waded through the crowd to the pantry, pulling open the door and searching for a can of beans. They're lying. Just ignore them.

"You will never have to go to school again!"

After a moment of searching, Max found the beans. He snatched them from the shelf, slamming the door shut and turning to the fridge. As fast as possible, he reached in for a cold can of Coke.

Think about Mario Kart…think about the tournament…

The aliens went silent for a split second. Then one shouted, "We can make Mario Kart real!"

Max's heart pounded. He turned on his heel, staring down at the miniature creatures. Mouth agape.

"You can read my mind?" he asked – then gasped, clamping a hand over the mouthpiece of his gas mask.

The aliens' big heads bobbed up and down on spindly necks. They swarmed him again, pressing tight against him. Touching his arms and legs. "Yes, yes! We can do anything you wish, young human!" They began to pull him. "Come with us!"

"No!" Max cried, trying to tear himself free. Their fingers suddenly became sticky, like glue. No matter how hard he tried, he was stuck. And the aliens were stronger than they looked; the ones holding his legs began to lift him off the floor, quicker than he could gain solid footing. "Let me go!"

"Come with us! We'll have so much fun together!"

Max wriggled and kicked, but it was no use; their glue-like grip was too strong. Suspended above their heads, the aliens took him through the kitchen and toward the front door. Through the window, Max saw a huge silvery object blocking out most of the starry night sky. Hundreds of little aliens gathered around it, chattering excitedly in a language he'd never heard before. A seam opened up on the side of the object – a ramp extended down, blazing light from within shining across the grass. Preparing to take him away.

Struggling as hard as he could, Max managed to get an arm loose. The can of Coke he held flew out of his hand, hitting the front door just as the aliens carrying him threw it open. It exploded open on impact, spraying the brown fizzy liquid everywhere – all over him and the aliens.

A terrible chorus of high-pitched shrieks erupted around him, and abruptly he was free. Max hit the floor, Coke running down his face as he looked up. The tiny little bodies once holding him aloft were quivering, slapping at their arms and bulbous heads. At first it looked like the gluey substance on their fingers was running – but on closer look, Max realized it was their greyish skin starting to melt. Bubbling like hot soup beneath the acidic carbonation.

Not waiting to see what happened next, Max leapt to his feet and bolted back into the kitchen. He unlocked the door as fast as his fingers would let him, slamming it shut behind him. Locking it back up and dashing downstairs. At the bottom step was his father, looking concerned.

"What happened up there?" he asked. "It took you a while…are you all right?"

Max nodded, heart pounding – not in fear, but excitement. "Yeah, everything's fine. Great, actually."

Dad frowned, eyeing him from head to toe. Taking in the soda dripping from his hair. "I take it you spilled my Coke?"

"It's for the best, probably," Mom chimed in from the kitchen. "You're addicted to that stuff." She appeared from around the corner, wiping her hands on her apron. When she saw Max's shabby appearance, she looked worried. "What happened to you, Max?"

Max couldn't help but grin, tearing off the gas mask. Licking up the soda that dribbled from his forehead to his lips.

"We're going to need more Coke."

THE WOLFMAN

Originally published in 'Legends of Night' by Black Ink Fiction (2021)

My father was terrified of wolves.

Even the most innocuous reference to them would set him off. His blue eyes would go wide and glassy; he'd quickly look away, pretend to be busy with something else. If anything about wolves was on television, he would change the channel – or shut it off entirely, even if the family was still watching. When the moon was full, clear in the night sky, he would always call in to work. Claim he had a headache and needed the sleep to recover. And on Halloween night, he never left the house. He would stay inside, keep the lights off and the doors tightly locked while my mother took Sarah and I trick-or-treating.

But we never thought it strange until the night the wolf howled.

Our house butted up against a thicket, nestled in the midst of a suburban area of the city. It was part of the schoolyard that ran the length of back yards in our neighborhood, fenced off to prevent the children from playing within it. As far as I had ever known, it housed only owls and birds of prey – never anything larger.

Yet, at dinner on that Saturday night, we all heard it. The deep, mournful howl of a wolf.

Father went pale. He looked up from his plate, eyes going wide. Attention focused solely on the large, curtained bay window that overlooked the backyard. Overlooked the thicket. His fork crashed to the table, slipping from trembling fingers.

"Honey—" my mother tried, but he was already in motion. He leapt to his feet, disappearing from the dining room at a run.

"Deanna, get the kids," he growled from somewhere down the hallway.

I shared a nervous look with my little sister. "Mom?"

Mother shook her head, but she put down her utensils and stood. Concern deepened the lines in her face. "Just get your shoes on. Help your sister."

Sarah and I left our dinners behind, doing as we were told. When Father returned from the bedroom, he was carrying a small, black case that I'd never seen before. But he said nothing; he only slipped his shoes on, grabbed a coat, and ushered us out into the chilly September night.

We spent that night at a hotel. Sarah and I shared the single bed with my mother, who quietly pleaded for my father to join us. But he refused. He sat in the recliner by the window, keeping the shades partly open. Watching. Waiting. Keeping the little black case by his feet at all times. He never slept.

Once we returned to the house, I finally worked up the courage to ask what was going on. As I came out of my room, at the time my father should have been leaving for work, I was surprised to hear him on the phone. He was arguing with someone. "I scheduled tonight off, Kelly. I scheduled it weeks ago." Dread filled his voice. "No, damn it, I can't come in."

I stood out of sight at the end of the hall, listening intently. Peering around the doorframe, finding my parents sitting on the couch beside the bay window. The curtains were open for a change; twilight cast pretty reds and golds across the deepening sky. Father glanced out the window, too – but not to admire the sunset. He stared at the moon, beginning to peek above the horizon.

"Well...okay, but the next time I request off in advance I better get it."

Mother looked concerned; her hand clasped his thigh.

"What did they say?"

Father tossed the cordless phone angrily down on the couch. Dragging his hands down his face. "Vince called in sick. No one else is available to cover that department except for me." His blue eyes hardened, taking in my mother deeply. "Kelly said I'd be fired if I didn't show up. He's starting to notice my habit of taking off once a month."

"It'll be okay, Grant." Mother's voice was soft, but she still looked scared. I didn't understand why. "We've gone several years without seeing anything. I don't think tonight will be any different."

Father didn't look convinced. His fingers tightened around hers.

"But if you do...promise you'll call me immediately."

"I promise."

I waited until my father left before I confronted my mother about what happened. She bit her lower lip, scanning my face. Angry that I had eavesdropped. But after a lengthy pause – in which she busied my sister with an art project in her bedroom – she sat back down on the couch with a heavy sigh.

"When your dad was a kid," she began, speaking in hushed tones. "He and his brother, your Uncle Bob, used to play in the thicket together. They would play hide and seek with each other out there. Then, one day, Dad saw something that scared him." Mother pressed her lips together. "When the fog rolls in from the river, sometimes it gets trapped in there, because of how thick the underbrush is. And because of that underbrush, it makes little peaks in the fog – peaks that look like animal ears." She paused, eyes darkening, before continuing. "Before Uncle Bob died, he used to scare your dad by telling him that a wolfman lived in the thicket."

"A wolfman?" I asked. "Like a werewolf?"

My mother nodded. "Bob used to tell him that the peaks in the fog were the wolfman's ears. To lock the doors and close the curtains if he ever saw them." She shook her head, eyes dropping. Turning back to the sewing project in her hands. "It was just a stupid story, made up by a bully."

"But we heard a wolf howl last night."

She didn't look up. "Maybe one of the neighbors was watching a movie."

"A wolf, a wolf!"

Mother hissed. A drop of blood splattered on the white linen in her lap, needle slipping from her grip and stabbing her finger. I turned; Sarah had appeared in the hallway, face beaming with excitement. She pointed toward the bay window, bouncing on her toes. "Mommy, Stephanie – there's a wolf in the thicket!"

Fear plunged my heart into my stomach. I turned back to my mother; she looked stony and upset.

"Sarah, were you standing there listening to us this whole time?"

Sarah's face dropped. She shook her head. "No, Mommy. I was in my room, like you said. I heard something outside, so I looked out my window." Her eyes lit up once again. "And there's a wolf in the thicket!"

Mother stood, sucking on her pricked finger and turning toward the bay window. "Well, let's have a look."

Sarah scampered across the living room to the rectangular glass. She stood on tiptoes, tapping it with her fingertip. Pointing toward the thicket.

"He's out there! Look!"

A thick fog had come in from the river, settling heavily across the schoolyard as night was just beginning to fall. The full, waxing moon rose above the horizon, casting dense shadow outward from the thicket's interior. Spreading across the top of the foamy, white cloud; a dark, eerie blemish. Just within the mouth of the thicket, beyond the roped off entrance, the fog was beginning to make peaks.

But there were only two. They faced the bay window, not shifting or swirling like the rest of the fog. The peaks were attached to something large and hulking, sitting on its haunches. Obscured by mist and shadow.

"See him? See the wolf?" Sarah giggled happily.

A chill fingered my spine. I turned to find Mother staring at the fog with a tight, pale face, fist clutching the collar of her dress. Blood slowly began to soak into its floral fabric from her untended finger.

"Get away from the window," she whispered urgently, pulling my sister back. She yanked the curtains shut, pushed us out of the living room and into the hallway. When the three of us were safely in my parents' bedroom – Mother locking the door – I began to panic.

"Mom, what's going on? What was outside?"

She ignored me, taking the phone from beside the bed and stabbing in a number on the dial pad. After a long pause, she spoke in a trembling voice.

"Grant, come home. Now."

"Deanna? What's wrong?"

"He's here," my mother breathed, eyes beginning to glisten.

Dead silence. Then, "I'm coming home right now. You know where I keep the bullets?"

She nodded, tears rolling down her cheeks. "Y-Yes."

"Then lock the doors and close the curtains. Hide the girls."

Once my mother hung up, I couldn't stop my own tears from flowing. "Mom, please tell me what's going on. Please!"

"Get under the bed, Stephanie." She threw open the closet door, reaching up to the highest shelf. She pulled something down from it – the little black case, from the night before. Something inside it made a metallic clatter as she slammed it on the dresser. "Keep Sarah close to you."

"Is it the wolfman?"

"I said get under the bed!" She tore the black case open. Metal glinted in the moonlight from the window; a pistol, clenched in her trembling fist. The magazine separated from the bottom of the handle, falling across her palm. She reached back into the case, beginning to load the magazine with bullets.

Silver bullets.

I sucked in a sob. Sarah was beginning to cry, too. "I th-thought you said the wolfman was just a stupid story!"

Mother snapped the magazine back into the pistol. She glared at me with wide, fearful eyes. Heading to the window and pulling the curtains shut. "Do as I say, Stephanie Louise!"

Clamping my mouth closed, I grabbed Sarah's hand, kneeling on the floor. I pushed my little sister under the bed, then slid in after her. Curling up at her side, I put my arm around her and squeezed her tight. Squeezed my eyes shut, stemming the tears – praying to God to keep us safe.

But, in the darkness of my thoughts, all I could see were the peaks in the fog.

***

Banging on the bay window began just as my father arrived home. It scratched and squealed, like nails on a chalkboard. I didn't dare to look; I kept my face to the fuzzy carpet, holding Sarah close. Doing everything I could to hold in the screams cramping my chest. Sarah shivered with sobs, but she didn't cry out. Perhaps she was too afraid to, like I was.

The front door opened and slammed. Heavy footsteps came to the bedroom door; a pounding knock rattled it in the frame. Mother shrieked.

"Deanna, it's me! Hurry!"

Mother's weight lifted off the mattress above us. The lock clicked, and the door swung open. Father's feet shuffled quickly inside.

"He's at the window. Where's the girls?"

"Under the bed," Mother whimpered. "Grant…."

The gun's safety clicked. The banging on the bay window grew louder.

"Stay here. I have to end this."

"But Grant, what if you miss? What if you...what if you can't go through with it?"

My father was silent for a long time. "I won't miss. I can't let him live like this anymore."

Glass began to shatter. A low, mournful howl filled the house, rattling the walls. Knocking the framed photo of our family off its hook. Father took a deep, shuddering breath. Then the bedroom door flew open again.

"Grant!" Mother screamed.

My father's footsteps thundered down the hall. His shout was lost to violent snarls and snapping jaws, the scrabbling of sharp claws on the hardwood floor. A braying howl that sounded vaguely human.

"Grraaaaaaannnntt!"

The gun fired twice; two loud claps of thunder. I squeezed my eyes shut. Something heavy crashed to the floor. Mother screamed again. Sarah began to wail. Then silence fell across the house, heavy and thick – like the fog the wolfman had come from.

"Deanna."

A relieved exhale exploded from my mother's lungs. She rushed down the hall. I turned to Sarah, brushing unruly blonde curls back from her quivering face. We didn't speak a word; we didn't have to. Our parents' relieved sobs from down the hall spoke volumes. Whatever they had been through, whoever the wolfman was to them...it was finally over.

I slid out from beneath the bed, encouraging Sarah to do the same. Taking her hand, we slowly stepped into the hall. Mother and Father stood in the living room, holding each other desperately. The pistol lay discarded on the floor, barrel still smoking. Mingling with the thick fog that poured in from the shattered bay window. Shards of glass caught the silvery light of the full moon, bright in the cloudless sky. It enveloped the twisted, mangled creature sprawled across the hardwood. Blood oozed from bullet holes in its chest; both piercing its heart.

"You did it," my mother sobbed, clutching my father close. "You killed him."

I couldn't take my eyes off the body of the wolfman. The closer I looked, the more it appeared human. Short snout, razor-like teeth, blood-stained lips and a blonde mane...blue eyes that stared emptily up into the moon. Blue eyes that looked just like my father's.

Father gazed down at us, extending a hand forward. A grim smile touched the corners of his lips. He pulled me to his side, arm falling around my shoulders tightly. Protectively. Sarah clutched my leg.

"It's over," he assured us softly, pressing my head to his hip. "He's gone."

"Who was he?" I asked.

"He was...." Father's eyes lingered on the stiff body; sadly, softly. "The wolfman."

***

My parents never again spoke of what happened that night in September. All four of us buried it deep – as deep as we buried the body of the wolfman. We laid him to rest in the mouth of the thicket, then forever turned our backs on that dark blot which stained our lives. Soon after, at the beginning of the following year, we moved far away from the city for a fresh start. But every now and again, as an adult, I would return home to visit.

It was only on his deathbed that my father broke his silence. Uncle Bob was his best friend, his mentor. He had never bullied his little brother. Uncle Bob had unknowingly run through wolfsbane in the thicket, getting pricked by its thorns as the brothers played hide and seek. He must have known what it was, and what it did; from that point forward, he spun the story of the wolfman, convincing my father never to play in the thicket again. When the hunger began to build, physical changes began to show, Uncle Bob warned my father. To keep the doors locked and the curtains closed. And to never let the wolfman see him.

Then he disappeared; to keep his little brother safe.

On the night of the full moon – the same night in September, thirty years after the wolfman was killed – I stood in the backyard of my abandoned childhood home, overlooking the thicket. The place from which our nightmare appeared. Dense fog was beginning to roll in from the river, glistening in the twilight that lengthened the shadows. It filtered through the trees, settling heavily atop the underbrush.

Making peaks, like animal ears.

ABOUT THE AUTHOR

T.L. Beeding was born and raised in West Sacramento, California. She wears many hats; a cancer survivor, a mother, a writer, and a proud Wiccan. She has written horrors for several publications, including Vanishing Point Magazine, Black Hare Press, and Eerie River Publishing. When she is not writing, T.L. enjoys seeking misadventures with her daughter, two cats, and boyfriend at their home in the Hudson Valley. She can be found on X at @tlbeeding, and through her website, www.tlbeeding.com.

Made in the USA
Middletown, DE
15 January 2025

68761233R00080